**Simon Brett** was educated at Dulwich College and Wadham College, Oxford, where he gained a First Class Honours Degree in English. A former radio and television producer, he has to date written over ninety books. A great many are crime novels, including the Charles Paris, Mrs Pargeter and Fethering series.

Simon was Chairman of the Crime Writers Association from 1986 to 1987 and of the Society of Authors from 1995 to 1997. He was President of the Detection Club from 2001 till 2015 and was awarded the 2014 CWA Diamond Dagger. He lives near Arundel in West Sussex and is married with three grown-up children, three grandsons, one granddaughter, and a cat called Polly.

## Also by Simon Brett

# BLOTTO, TWINKS AND THE HEIR TO THE TSAR

## Simon Brett

Constable • London

CONSTABLE

First published in Great Britain in 2015 by Constable

This paperback edition published in 2016

A CIP catalogue record for this book
is available from the British Library.

ISBN: 978-1-47211-834-9

Printed and bound by CPI Group (UK) Ltd, Croydon, CR0 4YY

Papers used by Constable are from well-managed forests and
other responsible sources.

MIX
Paper from
responsible sources
FSC® C104740

Constable
is an imprint of
Little, Brown Book Group
Carmelite House
50 Victoria Embankment
London EC4Y 0DZ

An Hachette UK Company
www.hachette.co.uk

www.littlebrown.co.uk

To Max,
With love from Papa

# Poor Relations

'It's absolutely the lark's larynx,' Blotto confided in the stable to his hunter Mephistopheles, 'being born with a whole canteen's worth of silver spoons in one's mouth. But if there is one major chock in the cogwheel to being an aristocrat, then it's the poor relations.'

Mephistopheles whinnied reassurance. Though horses of his breeding didn't actually have any poor relations, he was always ready to sympathise with his young master's troubles.

And it wasn't something that he had to do very often. Devereux Lyminster – universally known as Blotto – younger son of the late Duke of Tawcaster, was possessed of an emotional gamut that usually ran from 'Pretty Jolly Cheerful' to 'Deliriously Happy'. He wasn't much given to introspection. He left gloomy thoughts to intellectual types – clergymen, undertakers, poets and people like that.

Blotto had indeed been dealt a good hand in the poker game of life. His family history could be traced back to the Norman Conquest. He was blessed with extraordinary good looks, of the blond thatch of hair and piercing blue eyes variety. Though not aware of it, he was fatally attractive to women and when at Eton had inspired hero-worship in a whole generation of younger boys. The fact that his intellectual capacities made the average fruit fly look like a Regius Professor was not something that caused him any anxiety. He knew that if he got into some kind of glue pot where brainpower was needed, it could be readily supplied by his incredibly gifted sister, Honoria Lyminster – universally known as Twinks.

So long as Blotto didn't have to stir from the beloved environs of Tawcester Towers, and so long as he participated, according to the season, in plentiful amounts of hunting and cricket, he required nothing else of life. He possessed in abundance all the ingredients for happiness.

So Mephistopheles always noticed when his owner was in a less than sunny mood. He whinnied again to show solidarity and waited for the young master to reveal more confidences of which he, being a horse, would not understand a word.

'You see,' Blotto went on, 'every family has poor relations. It's just something that people of our class have to put up with – a bit like mumps or measles or chicken pox. You know, and you expect a few of the wretched pineapples to be hanging around at Christmas time. But they never stay long. The Mater sees to that.'

He knew whereof he spoke. Blotto's 'Mater', the Dowager Duchess of Tawcester, was not a woman to be underestimated. Carved from the living rock of history, since her husband the late Duke had died she had run the Tawcester Towers estate with a rod of iron. (As a matter of fact, she had done the same before her husband died. His will had never been a match for hers. His was always the velvet fist; hers the iron glove.)

Blotto and – to a lesser extent – Twinks had from birth been in awe of their mother. She had never believed in 'modern' ideas of mollycoddling her offspring. The Dowager Duchess's principles of childcare involved her seeing as little of her progeny as was humanly possible, delegating their upbringing to the brutal regime of a series of nurses and governesses. So effective had this approach been that when Blotto and Twinks appeared at their father's funeral, the Dowager Duchess did not recognise them and had to be introduced.

Her attitude to people outside the immediate family was even more frosty. Members of her own class existed only to be belittled. And when it came to poor relations, she was in her element. Her skills in patronising were legendary and she used them like a flamethrower. Not many of the poor relations who gathered at Tawcester Towers on Christmas Eve made it through to Boxing Day. Most, by then unable to resist the withering power of their hostess's insults, had scurried off back to their humble homes.

There was some proverb Blotto could never quite remember, about fish and guests starting to smell after three days. With his mother in charge of festivities very few invitees lasted even that long.

'You see, Mephistopheles,' his master went on, 'what makes the whole thing a bit of a candlesnuffer for boddoes in my sit is that you never know how many spoffing relations you've got. What you do know for sure is that it's a guinea to a groat that they'll be poor.

'It all goes back to the Middle Ages, when there were a lot of what were called "domestic" marriages . . .' He hesitated for a moment. 'I'm not sure that's the right word. 'Fraid I'm a bit of an empty revolver when it comes to words. No, "dynastic" – that's the one. That's the trout I should be tickling. Anyway, in these "dynastic" marriages, the sons and daughters of aristocrats were used like counters in a game of Ludo, shoved around the board and made to twiddle up the old marital reef knot with some other unlikely poor greengage with the right breeding. Wasn't to do with love or any of that rombooley – mind you, it very rarely is nowadays either for people of our class. You wouldn't believe the number of fillies the Mater has tried to get me trotting up the aisle with over the years. I've managed to escape the noose so far, but one day she'll have me collared.

'Anyway, back then – you know, in the Middle Ages, this "dynastic" marriage biz was just about increasing the size of their parents' estates – or in some circs, countries. Very rare to have an aristocratic wedding in those days where the bride and groom spoke the same language, let alone had anything else in common.

'Result is, people like us have got relations all over Europe, who might pop up at any moment like moles in the middle of the spoffing lawn. Which is what has happened with our latest unwanted visitors, the Bashuskys.'

Mephistopheles whinnied, perhaps acclaiming the fact that Blotto had finally got to the point. It was always difficult to know precisely what mental processes were going through that magnificent equine head.

'They're seventeenth cousins forty-three times removed or something vaguely round that map reference. And they're about as welcome as slugs in a shower. Four of them – Count Igor, Countess Lyudmilla and their bliss-bereft offspring, Sergei and Masha. Well, they got in touch with my brother ... you know, the Duke of Tawcester, though of course we always call him Loofah ... and said they were relations and Loofah thought for some reason that the decent thing would be to invite them down for a weekend. Which would all have been creamy éclair, had they left at the end of the weekend. Which they didn't. They stuck on like barnacles to a ship's bottom. And because they're family, we're expected to entertain the lumps of toad-spawn for as long as they choose to stay here.

'I keep saying they should go back to Russia, but for some reason apparently they can't go back to Russia.'

'The reason they can't go back to Russia,' announced an approaching voice that trilled like quicksilver, 'is because of the Revolution.'

Blotto looked round as his sister Twinks wafted in on a wave of more exquisite perfume than that to which the stable was accustomed. Her beauty was, as ever, flawless.

Hair so blonde as almost to be silver, cut in a fashionable bob, surrounded a perfectly shaped face whose ivory pallor was enlivened by the rose-red of her lips and the paler pink of her cheeks. Under the pleasing arches of her eyebrows sparkled a pair of azure eyes, whose colour darkened at times of high emotion almost to the depth of sapphires. Her slight figure was gracefully draped in a short dress of silver-grey silk above white silk stockings. She was the kind of iconic woman to elicit paeans of praise from sensitive poets. Though from the kind of people she met in her social circle she was more likely to hear cries of 'By jingo, you're a proper corker!'

Being her brother, Blotto of course didn't notice any of this. All he did notice was that, like his, her disposition had lost its customary sunniness. 'What's pulled your face down the wrong side, Twinks me old biscuit barrel?' he asked.

'It's Sergei,' she replied.

'Sergei Bashusky?'

'How many other Sergeis do you know?' she demanded with uncharacteristic pettishness.

'Not a great many,' her brother was forced to confess. 'Anyway, what's the stencher done to tweak your toenails?'

'He's fallen in love with me,' Twinks replied as though announcing some global epidemic.

'Oh, come on, me old frying pan, you ought to be used to that by now. Ever since I can remember, boddoes have been falling for you like giraffes on an ice rink.'

'I know, but none of them has been as persistent as Sergei Bashusky. He hangs on like a burr to a beagle's belly.'

'But I thought you were quite good at dampening down chaps' ardour, Twinks.'

'Yes, usually I can scrub 'em off my dance card with no twinges. But with Sergei it's different.'

'Is that because he's Russian?'

'Could be. Never the most cheery of races, I've heard. They'd take brollies to the French Riviera in August. So maybe that's what makes Sergei say what he says.'

'And what does he say?'

'He says if I don't love him as much as he loves me, then he'll coffinate himself.'

'Toad-in-the-hole!' said Blotto. 'What, so you don't come up with the silverware and then he'll string a rope over a rafter?'

'I think his favoured method is a revolver.'

'Well, I'll be jugged like a hare! What a wonky wheeze! Poor boddo's not even out of his teens, is he? Can't imagine why anyone would want to say "Goodbye, sunshine" at that age,' said Blotto with complete honesty. His mind could not encompass the idea of someone feeling so low as to contemplate such extreme measures.

'Mind you,' he said encouragingly, 'I've heard that a lot of boddoes who say that kind of globbins don't mean it. They're just crying fox.'

'Wolf,' said Twinks.

'Sorry? Not on the same page, me old bread bin.'

'The expression is "cry wolf", not "cry fox".'

'Oh, that's a bit of a rum baba.'

'Why?'

'Well, we don't have any wolves in this country, do we? Whereas we've got lots of foxes.' He patted the neck of his hunter affectionately. 'Though there soon won't be so many of them if Mephistopheles and I have anything to do with it.'

'Yes.' Twinks had long ago learnt that there were some conversations with her brother that were not worth pursuing, so she moved on. 'But the wasp in the jam in this case is that I don't know whether Sergei really means it or not. I mean, if I just dismiss his suggestion with a tinkling laugh and he goes on to pop some lead in his brainbox . . . well, I'm going to feel just the tidgiest bit responsible . . .'

'Guilty?'

'No, I didn't say "guilty". You should know, Blotto, that people of our class never feel guilty for anything they've done. Otherwise we couldn't maintain our fine historical traditions of mutilating serfs, making money from the slave trade and being rude to the servant class . . . oh, and waiters. Could we?'

'No,' her brother agreed. Then he had a thought. This was an event of such relative infrequency that he could never restrain a huge beam when it happened. 'I say, Twinks me old nailbrush, I've just had a buzzbanger of an idea.'

'What is it, Blotto me old china toothmug?'

'Well . . .' The beam spread further across his impossibly handsome face. 'If you were to say to Sergei Bashusky that his advances towards you are about as welcome as a snail in your salad and, so far as you're concerned, you'd like him to drop off the edge of the world . . .'

'Ye-es,' said Twinks cautiously. She'd heard too many of her brother's ideas over the years to be overly optimistic about their practicability.

'. . . then,' he went on, 'Sergei might well take his revolver to some quiet and out-of-the-way place . . . and coffinate himself!'

'I'm not sure that I—'

'Wait!' Blotto held up a hand to interrupt his sister. 'I haven't finished yet. Then all you have to do is get Count Bashusky to fall in love with you, then turn him down and – presuming these things run in Russian families, which they probably do – you tell him to strike his tents too, and he'll go off with a revolver to some quiet and out-of-the-way place and . . . So then you'd be two down. All you'd have to do next is to get Countess Bashuskaya and Masha to fall in love with you . . . then you turn them down . . . they go to some quiet and out-of-the-way place . . . they coffinate themselves and . . .' Blotto spread his hands wide in appreciation of his own genius '. . . we no longer have any of the Bashusky family getting under our feet and up our noses at Tawcester Towers!'

There was a long silence. Then Twinks said, 'Hm . . . But, Blotto me old windscreen wiper, do you really think that fits in with the Lyminster code, the principles of *noblesse oblige*? To behave as you suggest would be absolutely outside the rule book for people of our breeding.'

Blotto didn't contest what she said. Though he still thought his idea was a real buzzbanger, he could not resist the force of his sister's argument.

'Oh, broken biscuits,' he said, with the vehemence of the disappointed.

## 2

# Russian Gloom

'I want to go back to Moscow,' announced Masha, for maybe the fiftieth time that day. She stood by the mantel-piece, with one elbow on the marble surface and a cheek resting on her drooping hand. Her dress, highly fashion-able though it had been at the court of St Petersburg in 1917, was now faded and darned in many places. (Twinks, who was by nature generous, had suggested to her mother that she might offer her distant cousin some of the elegant cast-offs from her own wardrobe, but had received a characteristic rebuke from the Dowager Duchess who said, 'Great heavens, no! We don't want to encourage the stenchers.')

In similar pose, like a matching bookend, Masha's mother Countess Lyudmilla Bashuskaya, also had an elbow on the mantelpiece and a cheek resting on a droop-ing hand. Her dress too had a shabby, dated look, making her appear older than her years.

Either side of mother and daughter, again with elbows resting on the mantelpiece, stood Igor and Sergei Bashusky. The Count was wearing some kind of military uniform decorated with an excessive amount of Ruritanian frogging in tarnished gold. Across the expanse of his slightly grubby white waistcoat stretched a dull red sash, pinned to the material by some meaningless Romanov insignia. From his sagging bloodhound face a moustache trailed like disheartened wisteria.

Sergei's moustache was even less impressive. Blonder than his father's, his facial hair hardly registered. The fair semi-circle on his upper lip could have been the result of over-enthusiastic drinking of a cup of milk. It did not make him look older than his years – rather the reverse. His pimply face also bore witness to his extreme youth. So did his thin knobbly body, which seemed to be all elbows. He looked as though he was barely into his teens, let alone out of them.

And Sergei had clearly been a smaller lad when his clothes were tailored for him. Now his jacket was cramped across his shoulders and had no hope of being buttoned up across his chest. His discoloured beige trousers stood at half-mast up his legs, revealing between their ending and the top of his boots an expanse of much-darned and tightly suspended sock.

(Twinks had suggested helping the Count out with garments from her late father's wardrobe and offering Sergei some clothes which Blotto had grown out of, but again the Dowager Duchess had put the kibosh on the suggestion. 'If we let them start to feel comfortable here, Honoria, we'll *never* see the back of them.' And Twinks had to concede that her mother had a point.)

Masha let out another lengthy sigh before repeating, 'I want to go back to Moscow.'

Blotto was getting very sick of his distant cousin's moaning. From what he'd heard of Moscow, it sounded pretty much of a swamp-hole and how anyone could want to spend time there rather than at Tawcester Towers baffled his intellect (which, it has to be said, did not require a great deal to baffle it). Apart from any other considerations, everywhere else was 'abroad'.

He was also getting very sick of the Bashuskys hogging the fireplace in the Pink Drawing Room, where traditionally pre-prandial drinks were served by Grimshaw the butler. Tawcester Towers, in common with most aristocratic homes, had very little heating. In some of the favoured bedrooms fires were lit in the evening, but they had always died out by morning and residents and guests were used to waking up to frost on the inside of their windows and the water in their ewers frozen solid.

They were also used to plumbing that clanked through the night like some ghost army stirring after a century of sleep, to inefficient rose-adorned toilet bowls encased in mahogany boxes, and taps which rarely coughed up more than a few spits of unnervingly brown water. These were amongst the charms of the traditional English country house.

Yet another sigh burst from the tortured breast of Masha. 'I want to go back to Moscow,' she said (unsurprisingly).

Her mother picked up the mood. With a sigh even more elaborate than her daughter's, Countess Bashuskaya announced, 'I want to go back to Zoraya-Bolensk.'

This was at least a change of wished-for destination and Blotto might have welcomed the variety, were it not for the fact that Lyudmilla Bashuskaya had expressed the desire to return to the family estate of Zoraya-Bolensk almost as frequently as Masha said she wanted to go back to Moscow.

'At Zoraya-Bolensk,' she went on, 'we had everything we needed. Oh, how we enjoyed the unending summer days. How long we would spend sitting in the garden, with iced lemonade ... and of course samovar ...' She lapsed into mournful silence.

After a polite pause, Blotto asked, 'So what did they do?'

'I beg your pardon?'

'What did the people do?'

'I'm sorry?'

'You said, "And of course some of our ... " And then you stopped. I wanted to know what some of your people did.'

A puzzled furrow dug itself into the Countess's brow, and Twinks quickly interceded – as she had done so many

11

times in the past – to explain things to her brother. 'The expression she used, Blotto me old back-scratcher, was "samovar", not "some of our". She was referring to a Russian tea-making machine.'

'Machine, eh? I thought they had serfs to do everything for them in Russia.'

'The serfs were all emancipated in 1861,' said Twinks, who always knew that kind of stuff.

'Ah. Were they?' Blotto nodded sagely. Then he said, 'Emanci-whatted?'

'Freed.'

'Ah.' He nodded again. 'Good ticket,' he said approvingly.

'But some of the serfs,' Count Bashusky contributed, 'did not feel the need to be free.'

'Really?'

'Some were happy under the gentle yoke of their kind benefactors.'

'When you used the word "benefactors",' asked Twinks, 'do you mean "owners"?'

'Yes. At Zoraya-Bolensk the serfs were happy to serve us. There was a family who had been at Zoraya-Bolensk for generations, the Oblonskys. The head of the household was called Vadim Oblonsky, and his wife was called Galina. They and their many children worked for us, did everything for us. And no, of course they did not get paid. They did it for love.

'It was part of their tradition, an instinctive thing for them. They recognised that we were superior to them in every way and that it was an honour for them to work for us. That is the natural order of things.'

'What you say, Igor, is so true.' The Countess dabbed a patched handkerchief to her eye. 'I wonder how things are now at Zoraya-Bolensk . . .'

'We must not think of it,' said her husband. 'That way lies only more unhappiness.'

'You say I must not think about it, but there is nothing

else I can think about, from the misery of our exile in this God-forsaken country.'

Blotto was instantly incensed. He always got a bit vinegared off when people started criticising either his King or his Country. 'Now hold back the hounds a moment,' he said. 'You are talking about Great Britain, you know, which is not so much a "God-forsaken country" as "God's own country".' He looked curiously at the four Russians for a moment. 'I say, you don't by any chance play cricket, do you?'

'No,' they all agreed.

'I thought not,' said Blotto, his point made.

'But,' the Countess mourned on, 'it is impossible for my mind not to go back to Zoraya-Bolensk. This time of year it looks so beautiful under the snow, when frost outlines the branches of the cherry trees.'

'They will probably have cut down the cherry orchard,' said her husband lugubriously.

'No, I cannot bear it!' Countess Bashuskaya brought her free hand (the one that wasn't on the mantelpiece supporting her cheek) up to her brow. 'If I find out that they have cut down the cherry orchard, I will take my own life!'

'If you do that,' said the Count, 'I will not be able to survive without you. I will take my own life!'

Masha, who didn't want to be left out of the family aspirations, said, 'If I cannot go back to Moscow, then I will take my own life!'

Blotto looked across hopefully at his sister. Maybe a version of the solution he'd proposed to her in the stables might work after all . . . ?

But then Twinks was distracted by Sergei Bashusky saying, 'And if I do not win the love of Honoria, then I will take my own life!'

This was followed by a silence while Twinks looked up towards the ceiling in exasperation. Finally it was broken when Blotto, ever the genial host (even when he was entertaining guests who seemed unaware of what a great privilege it was for them to be at Tawcester Towers) said, 'Well, that's all tickey-tockey then.'

Grimshaw the butler circulated more drinks. It was noticeable that, in spite of their suicidal intentions, all of the Bashuskys had very healthy thirsts and appetites. Their presence was virtually doubling the Tawcester Towers victualling bills. And money was always a problem for the Lyminsters. Though Blotto and Twinks were continually going off on exploits of derring-do from which they returned loaded with loot, it got spent with amazing speed. Owning an English stately home was an expense of the scale of running a string of racehorses. It only took a collapsed roof in the East Wing or the death of a boiler for the cash to whoosh away like water down a plughole.

Nor did the local tradesmen show any awareness of the honour they were being granted by working for the aristocracy. Rather than the reduced bills and extended credit the Dowager Duchess and her ilk had grown up with, the modern-day artisans seemed actually to increase their prices for titled clients. And had a nasty habit of delivering final demands before they had sent out any other kind of demand.

The old respect for the Great and the Good was long gone. One of the few sentiments on which the Dowager Duchess of Tawcester and her unwanted guests might have agreed was a nostalgia for the days of serfdom. It was much more difficult to maintain a country estate now that everyone expected to be remunerated for their services.

And indeed, looking back in history, few of the world's famous monuments – the Pyramids, the Acropolis, the Colosseum – would survive if the people building them had expected to be paid. It was not everything, the Dowager Duchess frequently reflected – and here also the Bashuskys would have agreed with her – that had changed for the better. And indeed, when she brought her mind to focus on the subject – she couldn't actually think of anything that had changed for the better since her young days.

One striking feature of the group assembled for pre-prandial drinks in the Pink Drawing Room was the absence of the Dowager Duchess. It was quite common for her – and indeed her right – to appear later than her guests, leaving Blotto and Twinks to fulfill any hostly duties that might be required, but that particular evening the normal hour for the dinner gong to be struck had been passed by a good ten minutes and still there was no sign of the Dowager Duchess.

Twinks sidled across to Grimshaw to see if he had any explanation of her absence. He said he would dispatch Harvey, one of the older housemaids with whom he had a 'special' relationship, to make enquiries and left the room to find her.

He returned only moments later to confide to the young mistress that the Dowager Duchess was indisposed and would be taking a light supper in her bedroom.

Twinks was not fooled by this at all – nor indeed did it occur to her for a moment to worry about her aged parent's health. She knew full well that her mother would be ensconced in her bedroom with a couple of bottles of gin, listening to military marches on the gramophone.

It was a measure of how exasperated the Dowager Duchess was with the Bashuskys that she had taken this course. Normally the ingrained force of her breeding would make her sit through all kinds of grisly social events. Indeed people of her class never went to social events that were enjoyable. But that didn't normally stop them from attending. The fact that she had deliberately ducked out of another evening with her Russian cousins was a measure of how sick to death she was of them.

And when the Dowager Duchess was sick to death of a situation, she usually took speedy measures to bring it to an end. Twinks felt pretty sure that the next morning she and Blotto would receive a summons to attend their mother in the Blue Morning Room.

In the meantime, she and her brother had the unenviable task of managing a whole dinner of the Bashuskys without the welcome interpolations of their mother's patronising and belittling their guests.

As Grimshaw finally struck the gong and announced that dinner was served, Masha was heard to observe, with the inevitable sigh, how much she wished to get back to Moscow.

# 3

# The Dowager Duchess Makes a Stand

There are windswept crags at the extremities of various
landmasses to which the adjective 'forbidding' has frequently been applied, but none of them compare for sheer
cragginess to the face of the Dowager Duchess of Tawcester
when she's in a snit. And she was in quite a snit the following morning when she summoned her younger son
and daughter to attend her in the Blue Morning Room.

'Devereux,' she said, 'Honoria, something must be done!'

Blotto knew exactly what she meant, but still tried the
diversionary tactic of asking, 'About what?'

That ploy, however, was immediately blown out of the
water by his mother's roar of: 'About those four-faced
filchers the Bashuskys.'

'Ah yes,' said Blotto.

'Have either of you got a mouse squeak of an idea how
we can get rid of them?'

'Well . . .' Blotto began.

'I wasn't asking you, Devereux.'

'But you did say "either of you".'

'When I am looking for an idea and I say "either of you"
of course I am only referring to Honoria. You ought to
know that by now.'

'Good ticket,' murmured Blotto.

'So, Honoria . . . do you have any ideas?'

A furrow spoiled the perfect surface of Twinks's brow. Then, very tentatively, she suggested, 'Couldn't we just ask them to leave?'

Metaphorical thunder and lightning now played around the craggy surface of the Dowager Duchess's face. 'Honoria, how dare you suggest such a thing? After all that money and effort that was spent on your breeding. There are certain contractual duties that you have to take on automatically if you are born into our class, and one of them is the obligation to provide hospitality to one's relations.'

'Even one's poor relations?' asked Blotto.

'*Particularly* one's poor relations!' boomed the Dowager Duchess. When she was in this mood, to call her 'a tough old bird' would have been an insult to boiling fowl. 'However loathsome they are, however appalling their table manners and general deportment, *noblesse oblige* insists that they should be looked after in the ancestral home.'

'Is that true however badly the stenchers behave?' asked Twinks. 'Aren't there some kinds of actions that would have them hounded out like rats from the family vault?'

'What kind of actions?' asked her mother.

'Well, say a male guest has an unsuitably close physical encounter with his hostess – would that get them turned out?'

'Of course not, Honoria, don't be such a silly chit. That is how most aristocratic families have ensured the continuity of their line.'

'What,' suggested Blotto, 'if the guests stole something from their hosts?'

'That again,' said his mother, 'is a practice which has a long tradition in circles like ours. The theft of wives, daughters, armies and titles has been commonplace through the generations.'

'But what if . . .' Twinks proposed '. . . one of the guests actually killed his host or hostess? Wouldn't that be stepping over the line?'

18

'Great Wilberforce, no! That is part of the normal social interaction between people of breeding. A lot of it went on during the Wars of the Roses. I'm surprised, Honoria, that – given your supposed intelligence – you know so little of the history of families like ours.'

'Well,' asked Blotto, 'what kind of behaviour on the part of lumps of toad-spawn like the Bashuskys would justify seeing them off the premises with red ears?'

'Well, obviously, some lapse of protocol which might suggest that their aristocratic credentials are not up to snuff.'

'Like?' asked Twinks.

'Like using the wrong cutlery at the dinner table.' Oh, broken biscuits, thought Blotto, they're actually rather good at all that stuff. 'Like,' his mother went on, 'making their own beds or pouring drinks for themselves.' No, the Bashuskys didn't do that either. 'Like,' the Dowager Duchess concluded, 'treating the servants as their equals.'

Again no dice, thought Blotto. Though the Bashuskys were much more shabbily dressed than the meanest stable boy at Tawcester Towers, they still treated everyone below stairs with the proper contempt. There was no danger of anything nice being said about them in the kitchens. No, getting the Bashuskys out of his home, Blotto realised even more forcibly than before, was going to be a tough rusk to chew.

But there was still one glimmer of a possibility. 'Actually, Mater,' he said, 'Twinks and I were discussing one idea yesterday.'

'Oh yes? And what was that?' asked their mother in a manner that showed she had few expectations of the answer.

'Well, we thought it'd be rosettes for everyone if the Bashuskys all topped themselves.'

'And why might they take such an extreme course of action?'

'Ah, now this is where it gets clever,' said Blotto. His mother and sister exchanged looks. They knew that the word 'clever' used in any context related to Blotto inevitably involved an oxymoron. 'You see, that poor young droplet Sergei Bashusky has fallen for Twinks like a partridge stuffed to the gills with lead. She's told him his chances are rather less than those of a one-legged prize-fighter. Result is, the pot-brained pineapple has announced he's going to top himself. And I was just thinking that we only have to get all the other Bashuskys to fall for Twinks and we'll ... have ... a ... great ...' His mother's look seemed to draw out his breath like a vacuum pump and he had none left to articulate any more words.

The reptilian eyes of the Dowager Duchess flicked across to her daughter. 'Have you got any *sensible* ideas, Honoria?'

'Well, short of going to Limehouse to contract a gang of thugs to come here and strangle the lot of them, I don't have too many, no.'

The Dowager Duchess gave a peremptory shake of the head. 'We couldn't do that. It'd be against our code. We have a duty not only to welcome family members to Tawcester Towers but also to ensure their safety whilst they are within the estate boundaries.'

'Oh, tough Gorgonzola,' said Twinks.

A calculating look came into her mother's eye. 'On the other hand ... if we were to get someone to take the Bashuskys up to Limehouse and introduce them to the thugs ... well, the Lyminsters would have no responsibility for what happened to them there.'

Twinks pursed her lips. 'The only chock in the cogwheel there, Mater, is that – as you may have noticed – the Bashuskys never seem to want to go anywhere. We've suggested many expeditions which might get them off the premises, but they've turned down all such suggestions. All they seem to want to do is stay inside Tawcester Towers.'

'Eating our food and drinking our liquor,' said the Dowager Duchess peevishly. 'You're right, Honoria. And if we had someone kidnap them and take them off to Limehouse . . . well, once again we'd be offending against the Lyminster code of hospitality.'

'Yes, isn't that just the flea's armpit?' Twinks observed ruefully.

There was a silence. Then her brother said suddenly, 'Toad-in-the-hole! I've had a real bingbopper of an idea!'

His mother and sister once again looked towards him with low expectations. 'What is it, Devereux?' asked the Dowager Duchess.

'Well, I was thinking – and when you hear it you'll really have to admit that it's a beezer idea – that whereas the Bashuskys being coffinated by hired thugs might look a tidge suspicious, *accidents* can happen to anyone.'

He sat back for a moment, pleased with his revelation, but his mother chivvied him, 'Your point being?'

'Well, if I were to arrange a shooting party for all of the Bashuskys and set up for them all to be killed . . . you know, the Count could get hit while one of the staff was reloading his gun, there could be some obstruction in the barrel of the Countess's which blows her off on the quick route to the Pearlies. Then similar accidents happen to Masha and Sergei and . . .' Blotto spread his hands wide '. . . *problemo solvo.*'

'Hm,' was all that his mother said. A dark cloud of thought had settled around her craggy forehead.

So Blotto reinforced his case. 'I mean, like I say, accidents can happen, particularly in shooting parties. If Lord Tewkesbury hadn't tripped while looking down the wrong end of his shotgun, the Tensington Castle estate wouldn't have been inherited by an Italian gigolo. Apart from that, just think of the number of beaters who get inadvertently shot during the average Tawcester Towers shooting season. And no one ever makes any fuss about them, do they?'

'Well, except for their families,' said Twinks.

'Yes, except for their families,' Blotto conceded. 'But no one important. We see the widows get tossed a few sovs and invite them for a glass of sherry on Christmas morning – for which they are as pathetically grateful as befits their station – but nothing else happens. No police investigation or any of that diddle-doddle.'

The grey cloud of thought now darkened around the Dowager Duchess's brows. Then she pronounced her verdict. 'I like the way you're thinking, Devereux. That idea is by far the most sensible I've heard from you since you gave up short trousers. But I believe that, beneath the structure of your plan there is a flaw.'

'Well, there's a floor beneath most things, Mater,' Blotto pointed out. 'If you're indoors, that is.'

'That was not the kind of "flaw" to which I was referring, Devereux.'

'Oh, fair biddles then.'

'Though I like your suggestion a great deal . . .' Blotto beamed '. . . I fear that while the accidental death of one of the Bashusky family could be reckoned to be merely unfortunate, the accidental deaths of all four might require a level of coincidence which could not fail to attract the interest of the local police force.'

'Don't don your worry-boots about that, Mater. The local police force round here are represented by Inspector Trumbull and Sergeant Knatchbull of the Tawcestershire Constabulary. I've heard you say many times that they couldn't investigate their way out of bed. Their only role in such proceedings is to be permanently baffled.'

'That is indeed true, Devereux. But I still believe that the accidental deaths of four members of the one family in the same shooting party would cause comment. And comment of the kind that might lead to gossip at Hunt Balls and other social functions.'

'Oh, and we can't allow that to happen, can we, Mater?' said Twinks with an edge of irony in her tone.

But such nuance was lost on the Dowager Duchess. 'No, we certainly cannot!' she boomed. 'But we must find a way to remove these leeching limpets, the Bashuskys! Have you never heard them mention anywhere else they would like to spend the rest of their lives – other than here at Tawcester Towers?'

'Well,' said Blotto, 'Masha does keep cluntering on wanting to go back to Moscow.'

'Oh?' The Dowager Duchess's antennae were instantly alert.

'And,' Twinks agreed, 'they do all keep saying how much they wish they were back in Russia.'

'Then the solution is simple,' the Dowager Duchess announced. 'We must take them back to Russia!'

'Must we?' asked Blotto with some foreboding.

'Yes,' his mother confirmed. 'And when I say "we", of course what I mean is "you two".'

# 4

# More Brainpower Brought on Board

'Are you telling me that you've never heard of the Russian Revolution?'

'Yes,' replied Blotto. There were certain aspects of his personality that could perhaps be criticised, but no one had ever questioned his honesty.

Professor Erasmus Holofernes ruffled his hands in amazement through his grey curls, making them stick out in all kinds of new directions. As an academic moving in the rarified Senior Common Room circles of St Raphael's College, Oxford, he had always believed that ignorance was finite, that at some point plumbing its depths would discover the bottom. But that was before one of the few people he sometimes regarded as his intellectual equal, Honoria Lyminster, had introduced him to her brother.

'Do you know anything about international politics?' asked the Professor.

Another easy one. 'No,' said Blotto.

Erasmus Holofernes looked in bewilderment around his room. It was, as ever, a post-Armageddon landscape of scattered paper, every surface so covered that one could only guess at what furniture might lie beneath the confusion. The Professor had instinctively homed in on something solid to sit on (perhaps a chair) behind a particularly high pile of documents (perhaps a desk). Twinks too had found a more or less stable perch. Blotto, distrustful of the tottering heaps of paper all around him, had chosen to remain standing. He noticed that the piles on the sills had grown so high that soon no natural light would be allowed in through the leaded windows.

'Maybe, Prof,' he suggested, 'you could give me the SP on this Russian Revolution caper? Then we'll all be on the same page.'

Professor Erasmus Holofernes sighed heavily and looked across at Twinks, whose azure eyes encouraged him to provide her brother with an explanation.

'Very well,' he conceded. 'The Russian Revolution of October 1917 was in fact the culmination of a series of lesser revolutions. One of them had taken place earlier that year, in March – that was called "The February Revolution". Then—'

Blotto didn't reckon he'd get many opportunities to correct the great Professor Erasmus Holofernes on a point of error, so he quickly said, 'I think you've got a bit of a fluff-up in your facts, me old poached egg. If this revolution business took place in March then it should have been called "The March Revolution". Easy mistake to make, but I thought you'd thank me for pointing it out.'

The Professor's eyes bulged out of their sockets. Many undergraduates and doctorate students had sat in that room. Before that day none had ever dared to question him on a point of fact.

'The reason,' he barked, 'why "The February Revolution" is called "The February Revolution" is that, though the date was March in Great Britain, it was February in Russia. The difference being due to the fact that while our country had progressed to using the Gregorian Calendar, the Russians were still using the Julian Calendar. Have you heard of either of those?'

'No,' Blotto readily admitted.

'Well, the Gregorian Calendar is so called because it was introduced by Pope Gregory XIII in 1582. Now the former Julian Calendar had been . . .'

He became aware of rather pointed throat-clearing from Twinks and looked across to her for its cause.

She smiled with all the tact and charm she could muster (a considerable amount – England is still littered with young men whose lives had never recovered from receiving the full beam of her azure eyes). And she said, 'I think, if you don't mind, Razzy, could you chop off all the ivy and just give us the chapter headings?'

'But the Russian Revolution is not the kind of subject that can be understood without a sense of its context. I mean, it'd be meaningless to someone who can't tell the difference between a Menshevik and a Bolshevik.' He faced Blotto squarely. 'What is the difference between a Menshevik and a Bolshevik?'

'Ah,' came the reply, 'I'm not terribly good at riddles. But something tickles the old memory glands between a prison guard and a watchmaker, I think.'

'What you mean,' Twinks helped him out, 'is: "What is the difference between a jeweller and a jailor?"'

'Exactly. Give that pony a rosette! And the answer was . . . ?' However many times he'd been told the riddle, the pay-off always somehow seemed to slip out of the old brainbox. Once again he looked to his sister for help.

Which she supplied. '"One sells watches and the other watches cells."'

'Bong on the nose, yes! Another rosette for the pony!'

'I'm sorry,' said Professor Erasmus Holofernes severely, 'but I fail to understand what any of this has to do with the difference between a Menshevik and a Bolshevik. Have you ever heard of either a Menshevik or a Bolshevik, Blotto?'

Ah, back to the easy questions, he thought with relief. 'No,' he replied, his honesty again exemplary.

'Well, Twinks, your brother has a great deal to learn about the Russian Revolution. Without a knowledge of the Romanov regime, of the 1905 Revolution, the Emancipation of the Serfs in 1861, the assassination of Alexander II and—'

'Take those as read. Give him the banner headlines.'

'I'm not sure I can do that,' said the Professor, somewhat aggrieved. 'It goes against my every instinct as an academic. Banner headlines are the province of minor intellects like journalists.'

'Well, look, Razzy, would you mind if *I* were to give Blotto a two-line summary of the Russian Revolution, so that he knows the basics, and then we can move on to the real purpose of our meeting.'

'Very well,' said Holofernes grumpily. 'Though the idea that any sensible explanation of the Russian Revolution can be done in two sentences is frankly laughable.'

'No harm in letting me have a biff at the bootjack, though, is there?'

He conceded there wasn't.

'So, tune up the eardrums, Blotto me old carpet brush, and I'll tell you what happened during the Russian Revolution.' Her brother looked appropriately alert, as she went on, 'Russia used to be run by an imperial monarchy and lots of rich aristocrats whose every need was looked after by downtrodden serfs.'

'In other words, like any other civilised country,' Blotto observed.

'Don't interrupt her,' said the Professor. 'Twinks, you only have one sentence left to encapsulate the immensity of this major political process.'

'I know,' said Twinks with an infuriating smile. Then she turned back to her brother. 'Second sentence,' she announced. 'In 1917 the common people took over the government, the Emperor abdicated; a year later he and his entire family were shot dead.'

'That's two sentences!' crowed Professor Erasmus Holofernes.

'No, it isn't,' Twinks crisply snapped back. 'The two thoughts were separated by a semi-colon, not a full stop.'

'I don't think using semi-colons is fair.'

'Well, you should have made the rules clear before I delivered the sentences.'

The two combatants eyed each other in defiant silence. Though this was the kind of intellectual horse-trading they both enjoyed, Twinks recognised it wasn't the moment for such self-indulgence. She turned to her brother. 'So has that lifted the mist a bit, Blotto me old rubber bath plug?'

'Yes, it has, by Wilberforce! And what a fumaciously sticky glue pot those Ruskies have got themselves into. This is what happens, you know, when boddoes try to repair something that doesn't need repairing. Just the same as here in good old Blighty, where the feudal system had worked perfectly for ages until some so-called reformers came and threw a kettle into the cogs. I mean it's against the spoffing laws of nature to have serfs in charge of things. To have the upper classes on top makes perfect sense. Why else are they called "upper", after all? That's the way God designed things to be in God's own country.'

This was possibly the longest uninterrupted speech Blotto had ever delivered and when he came to the end of it he felt as surprised by his eloquence as did his audience.

Then the Professor said, 'We may be living in God's own country over here, but is Russia also God's own country?'

'Ah,' said Blotto. 'You're bang on the bull's eye there, Prof. Obviously God, being British, puts most of His beef into looking after us here. But He has a famously kind nature, so I'm sure He's still quite generous to boddoes who have the misfortune to be born foreign. Anyway, what sort of religion do they have in Russia? Do they have lots of bells and incense like the Rock Cakes?'

'Rock Cakes?' echoed a bewildered Professor.

'R.Cs. Roman Catholics.'

'Ah. No. They have the Russian Orthodox Church.'

'Do they, by Denzil?'

'Well, rather they did. The new Communist regime wants to get rid of the Church altogether.'

'Do they? The stenchers! Don't the rats' tails have any respect for tradition?'

'No, that's exactly what they don't have.'

'Well, it sounds a pretty wocky business to me. I've always thought the Church should be, sort of . . . sacred.'

It was perhaps surprising that Blotto should produce such a stalwart defence of his country's established religion, since he had no faith at all. True, for most of his life at Tawcester Towers and at Eton he'd attended chapel at least once a week, but he'd never believed a single word of any of it. On the other hand, he was fortunate in the religion in which he had been brought up. For members of the Church of England, details like lack of belief had never been that important.

Though Twinks had listened with interest to the unusual sound of her brother engaged in theological debate, she now thought it was time for the conversation to move on. 'Anyway,' she asked Blotto, 'you have now got the basics of the Russian Revolution locked in the old brainbox, have you?'

'I certainly have. And a right pigsty's floor it sounds. No respect for tradition.' He shook his head at the awefulness of the thought.

'The Bolsheviks,' said Twinks, 'have even changed the name of the imperial city of St Petersburg.'

'Have they, the stenchers?'

'First they called it Petrograd and now Leningrad.'

'What fumacious names!'

'I'm in the same pigeon-hole as you there, Twinks. St Pertersburg sounds much nicer.'

'And for the majority of White Russians,' said Professor Erasmus Holofernes, 'it will always be St Petersburg.'

29

'Of course it will.' Twinks turned to her mentor. 'Right, Razzy, what about our little problemette? What odds do you reckon we have in the Getting-the-Bashuskys-back-to-Russia Stakes?'

'Absolute zero,' the Professor replied. 'There might have been a chance while the Civil War was going on that things could return to some version of normality. But the Whites were so comprehensively beaten by the Reds that the Bolsheviks have now got their hands on power in a grip which won't be easily relinquished.'

'Oh,' said Blotto. He couldn't think of another response which wouldn't reveal he had no idea what the Professor was on about.

Sensing his bewilderment, Twinks chipped in with an explanation. 'The Reds are the Communists who have taken over the country, Blotters, while the Whites are the supporters of the old imperial regime.'

'So the Whites are our sort of people and the Reds are oikish spongeworms?'

'Yes, that pretty well covers the table.'

'Good ticket.' Blotto paused for a moment. 'So the Bashuskys are . . . ?'

'White.'

'Oh.' Blotto rather regretted his use of the expression 'our sort of people'. It was not a category in which he would have wished to include the unwelcome guests at Tawcester Towers. 'So most of these White boddoes are still in Russia, are they?'

'No,' replied Professor Erasmus Holofernes. He wasn't used to not being part of a conversation on his home turf for so long. 'The Whites who didn't manage to get out were all killed. The rest emigrated.'

'Where to?'

'Throughout Europe. There are substantial White Russian communities in Berlin and Paris.'

'And a smaller one at Tawcester Towers.'

30

'Ah.' Understanding flooded Blotto's face like an opening daisy. 'So the Bashuskys are White Russians!'

'Your sister just told you that,' said the Professor testily.

'Yes, but he's got it now,' said Twinks. 'You're bong on the nose, Blotters.'

'Toad-in-the-hole, yes! I see it all now!'

'Thank the Lord for that,' the Professor muttered with a mix of exasperation and relief.

'So, Razzy,' asked Twinks, 'do you have contacts for the expatriate White Russian community in London?'

'Of course I do,' he replied. He would have felt insulted if anyone else had asked him the question, but he always made special rules for Twinks. He reached into an apparently random pile of papers and extracted three collections of documents held together with treasury tags. As he handed them across, he itemised them. 'London. Berlin. And Paris. I also have lists for Rome, Geneva and Madrid.'

'This lot'll do for the time being,' said Twinks.

'So, to tie the final bow on the Christmas parcel,' said Blotto, keen to demonstrate that he was keeping up, 'all we have to do is get the horracious Bashuskys back to Russia. Once we've done that, it'll all be creamy éclair!'

'Not exactly,' said Holofernes, waving an admonitory finger. 'You are talking about a very violent regime. They have murdered many people.'

'What kind of people?' asked Blotto.

'White Russians.'

'Well, we're not spoffing White Russians, so we should be safe.'

'They hate aristocrats.'

'Oh, that's not so good for us, Prof.'

'They have also killed many of the intelligentsia.'

'Ah,' said Blotto, his brow clearing. 'So I should be all right then.' One of his more endearing qualities was self-knowledge.

'Maybe. But think of the danger your sister will be in.'

'Ah yes. Fair biddles. So there might be the odd problemette getting the Bashuskys back to their home territory?'

'The only way what you want could be achieved is by turning back history. For people like the Bashuskys to be safe in Russia you'd have to undo everything that has happened there in the last decade.'

'You mean,' asked Twinks, 'we will have to rewind the events of the Russian Revolution and its aftermath?'

'Exactly,' the Professor confirmed.

'Well, if that's what needs to be done,' said Blotto with characteristic mindless bravado, 'then that is what we'll spoffing well have to do!'

# 5

# A Consultation with Corky Froggett

Of the four things in his life that Blotto loved, only one was human. And that was his sister Twinks. The other objects of his unvacillating adoration were his cricket bat, his hunter Mephistopheles and his Lagonda.

The pecking order between the three sometimes varied a little. In rare (very rare) moments of introspection he might occasionally think he cared more for his cricket bat than his hunter. But it only took one reproachful look from Mephistopheles's black eyes for him to feel guilty about his disloyalty and reverse the hierarchy.

In the same way, when he was opening up the throttle of the Lagonda and sending his social inferiors scuttling into the hedgerows of Tawcestershire's narrow lanes, the car had to be his primary source of joy. But then when he returned it to the garages, he sometimes felt a pang of regret for neglecting to have thought about his cricket bat or his hunter for such a long time.

But these were only minor ruffles on the habitually smooth surface of Blotto's disposition. Most of the time he loved his cricket bat, his hunter and his Lagonda with equal adoration.

So, after breakfast the morning following his trip to St Raphael's College, Oxford, Blotto found his footsteps turning instinctively towards the Tawcester Towers garages.

There, as he did most mornings, he would witness the ritual of the Lagonda being cleaned by his faithful chauffeur.

Corky Froggett was a man of army background, meticulous in all aspects of his life. For him the cleaning of the Lagonda took on the outlines of a military operation. But then everything he did took on the outlines of a military operation. Getting out of bed, washing and shaving, dressing in his chauffeur's uniform, eating breakfast – Corky Froggett had completed an entire campaign before he got near to his workplace in the Tawcester Towers garages.

Every morning Blotto loved to lean against the garage door frame, light up a cigarette and watch Corky in action. He found reassurance in the unvarying way the chauffeur laid out his extensive store of cleaning equipment and the unchanging order in which he approached the various parts of the Lagonda. The fact that on many mornings – and particularly in the summer when the car had often not been taken out of the garage all day – it did not need cleaning did not deter Corky Froggett from his self-imposed duty.

At the end of the ritual, with a nonchalant cry of 'Well done, Corky', Blotto would ease himself away from the garage door and move on to his next port of call, which was usually the stables to visit another object of his adoration, Mephistopheles.

But this particular morning he stayed to engage the chauffeur in conversation. 'Wondered, Corky old kipper, whether you'd had any more stirrings amongst the grey cells about the Lag's secret compartment . . . ?'

This was a frequent topic of conversation between them. During an adventure in the United States of America Blotto's Lagonda had suffered the indignity of being stolen by a group of Chicago gangsters. While it was in their custody, the chassis of the vehicle had been converted to include a hidden storage space which could accommodate two bodies (alive or, more frequently in Chicago, dead).

Though offended by the sacrilegious treatment of his Lagonda's sacred bodywork, Blotto had come to realise the advantages of the car's new feature. The job had been expertly done, so that no one inspecting the car would ever be able to see where the entrance to the compartment was. Its hidden space had enabled Blotto to smuggle out of America a large amount of bullion which had turned around the financial fortunes of Tawcester Towers. And when that bullion had been purloined and taken to Egypt, Blotto and Twinks had used the same hiding place to drive it safely back from there to England. So while the purist in Blotto (and in Corky Froggett, who was at least as obsessed with the car as his master was) felt that the Lagonda should be returned to the pristine state in which it had left the factory, there were times when he was all too aware of the advantages of the secret modification.

And that morning was one of those times. 'You remember when we last had a gab about the old secret compartment, Corky?'

'Certainly do, Milord.' The chauffeur stood to attention, as he always did when not actually bending down or asleep (and he slept horizontally at attention). 'It was last Tuesday morning.'

'And then, as I recall, I said the best ticket would be to whip the thing out like a wobbly tooth.'

'That is exactly what you said, Milord.' He gestured to the contents of four toolboxes neatly lined up on the garage floor. 'And I was about to start the dismantling process as soon as I'd finished the morning's car cleaning. Which is now.'

'Yes, well, rein back the roans for a moment, Corky. I've swapped horses on that particular hurdle.'

'Very good, Milord.' If he regretted the young master's change of mind, under no circumstances would the chauffeur have allowed his expression to show the fact.

'I think we may well be off on our travels again soon, Corky, and I don't need to tell you what a chitterling-saver that compartment has been to us in foreign parts.'

'You don't indeed, Milord.'

'So I was thinking, I'm not sure of the standard of filling stations available where we're pongling off to, and it might be tickey-tockey if we were to fill up the secret compartments with jerrycans full of petrol to keep the old Lag going in foreign climes.'

'Excellent thought, Milord.'

'Apart from anything else, Corky, I'd rather fill the lag's tank with English petrol than the kind of globbins they sell abroad.'

'Excellent idea, Milord.' Corky Froggett didn't think it was the moment to tell the young master that all the petrol bought in England had been imported from elsewhere, so didn't really justify his chauvinism.

There was a brief silence before the chauffeur asked, 'Is this a foreign trip that might involve myself, Milord? I don't need to tell you that I will happily be posted on your behalf to any vile and mosquito-ridden outpost of the known world.'

'I know you will, Corky. You've always been a Grade A foundation stone. And yes, I think you'd better come along with us.'

'Us? Is your sister to be involved, Milord?'

'She spoffing well is.'

'Excellent, Milord. Is the destination involved a dangerous one?' asked Corky eagerly.

'I'd say it very definitely is.'

'Your answer is meat and drink to me. And you know if ever I find you in a situation of mortal danger, Milord, I will regard it as a privilege to save you by interposing my own body between yourself and the attacking bullet, blade or other means of assault.'

'I know that, Corky.'

'Nothing would give me more satisfaction than to lay down my life in the service of my young master. I feel I was only spared in the last little dust-up with the Hun so that I would still have a life to sacrifice in the greater cause of your protection.'

'That's very four-square of you, Corky.'

'I will fully understand, Milord, if the answer to my question is to be kept under wraps, but might I ask to what country our latest expedition is to take us?'

'Russia,' Blotto replied dramatically.

'Russia, eh?' A twisted grin appeared beneath the upright bristles of Corky Froggett's moustache. 'Oh yes, the Ruskies were involved in our last little set-to with the Boche.'

'And did you coffinate any of them?' asked Blotto, knowing that his chauffeur tended to grade foreign countries according to how many of their nationals he had killed.

'No,' came the somewhat wistful reply.

'And why was that?' asked Blotto, genuinely surprised.

'Ah well, you see, Milord, in that particular little spat the Ruskies were on the same side as we were.'

'Really?'

'Yes. Against the Hun. Or at least they were meant to be.'

'Sorry, not on the same page?'

'The history of war, Milord, is littered with examples of allies turning out to be not as friendly as they were meant to be. So if someone says they're your ally, that is a warning to be on your guard. Fix your bayonet and wait for the attack.'

'Toad-in-the-hole,' said Blotto. 'And the Ruskies were like that?'

'Very untrustworthy, Milord. But so long as they were described as our allies, certain formalities had to be observed.'

'So you're saying that at that time killing them would have been outside the rule book?'

'Absolutely, Milord. Terribly bad form. Also quite difficult.'

'Oh?'

'Because we was never likely to meet any of them. You see, we was attacking Germany's Western front while the Ruskies was attacking on their Eastern border. So there was this whole land mass between us, full of sausage-munchers. Which meant, with regard to encountering any Ruskies, we was defeated by geography.'

'Oh, so was I,' said Blotto in heartfelt tones, remembering the terrible torturing tedium of Geography lessons at Eton. 'So,' he went on, 'you've never even met a Russian?'

'Except for the current houseguests at Tawcester Towers, no, Milord.' For a moment he seemed undecided whether to continue, then said, 'Mind you, I've heard quite a lot about them and from what I gather your average Ruskie is something of a slippery eel.'

'Really?'

'Oh yes, Milord. And if I ever found one trying to cheat myself or a member of your family, it would give me great pleasure to shoot him dead.'

'Well, maybe you'll get the chance on this little jaunt,' said Blotto encouragingly. 'From what I gather from some brainy boddo in Oxford, the Russians are no longer our allies.'

'Really, Milord,' said Corky Froggett, a twinkle of blood lust already sparkling in his eye.

'No, they've had some kind of Revolution, apparently.'

'So they're our enemies?'

'Um . . .' Blotto was a bit confused by all the details he'd so recently heard from Professor Erasmus Holofernes.

'So,' Corky pressed his point, 'if I were to shoot all of the Bashuskys, I would only be doing my duty as a member of His Majesty's armed forces?'

Blotto's fine mouth twisted in an expression of annoyance. 'Sadly that wouldn't fit the pigeon-hole, no. It seems there were two sides in this Revolution, the Munchybix and the Bulkybix or something. Black and White – no, sorry, Red and White. And it seems the Reds are against us . . .'

'So it's all right to shoot them?'

'Oh, yes, if you did that, you'd be doing the decent doings for King and Country.'

'So, if I shoot the Bashuskys . . .'

Blotto shook his head ruefully. 'No biddles. They're White Russians.'

'They don't wear any uniform to say that, do they?'

'No, Corky, they don't.'

'So it might be all right for a small mistake to be made, for them to be shot in error?'

'Oh, I wish climbing one's way out of this treacle tin was that simple. No, if the lumps of toad-spawn were to be shot while they're at Tawcester Towers . . .'

'Well, I could take them away from Tawcester Towers.'

'Still'd reflect badly on the Lyminster standards of hospitality.'

'Oh, snickets!' said the chauffeur. It was rarely that he used strong language in front of the young master, though on this occasion he had been sorely provoked. (When he was not in the company of the young master of course he swore like the trooper he had once been.)

'No, I'm afraid the only way out, Corky me old mucker, is to make the trip to Russia, where of course,' Blotto continued encouragingly, 'all of the boddoes in power are Reds, so you can shoot as many of them as you like.'

Corky Froggett nodded. He would have preferred to go out and shoot the Bashuskys straight away, but the prospect of deferred gratification was better than none at all.

'Now there is one knuckle-cracker we have to sort out,' Blotto went on. 'When we set off on this frolic we'll be taking the Bashuskys with us.'

'Oh dear. Why on earth do we want to do that, Milord?'

'Because the bull's eye in this particular shooting match is to take them into Russia and come back without them.'

'What, so as soon as we get across the border we hand the Bashuskys over to the Reds and let them do the shooting?' Corky couldn't keep the disappointment out of his voice.

'No there are a few more kinks in the fly-line before that. But don't let's don our worry-boots about them right now. There's a practical problem we have to solve.'

'What's that, Milord?'

Blotto looked fondly at his splendid car, whose dark blue bodywork glowed from the chauffeur's recent attentions.

'The Lag is a wonderful beast, and we could get six passengers in for a short trip without luggage, but not halfway across Europe. We'd never get all the Bashuskys in as well as you, me, Twinks and all our luggage ... even if we stuffed a couple of them into the secret compartment.'

'No,' Corky agreed.

'So how do we get round that particular poser?'

'Might I suggest, Milord,' said the chauffeur with appropriate deference, 'that we take a second car?'

'What a bingbopper of an idea!' said Blotto. 'Give that pony a rosette! We've got plenty of cars in the garages here. What do you recommend we take? One of the Rollers?'

Corky Froggett looked thoughtful and somewhat gratified. He liked it when the young master appealed to his expertise in the matter of automobiles. And in the matter of killing people, though that subject came up less frequently. 'I think,' he opined after a moment of assessment, 'that though the Rolls-Royces are undoubtedly fine machines, they might be outpaced by the Lagonda on the open road.'

'Ah, good ticket,' said Blotto, who hadn't thought of that.

'So my recommendation, Milord, would be that the Bashuskys are driven in one of the Hispano-Suizas. Though obviously not such supreme feats of engineering as the Lagonda ...' Blotto chuckled at the incongruity of the idea '... the Hispanos are still pacey little motors.'

'Hoopee-doopee!' said Blotto. 'The Hispano it is!' He was silent for a moment. 'Question is: who do we get to drive the thing?'

Corky Froggett's face lengthened. Though undoubtedly a team player – as his service during the recent unpleasantness with the Boche had demonstrated – he could not pretend to have a very high opinion of other members of his own profession. It was his view that the only half-decent driver in the Tawcester Towers vicinity – except of course for the young master – was one Corky Froggett.

'I'm sorry, Milord,' he said. 'I am afraid there is no one on the staff capable of undertaking such a challenging task.'

# 6

# The Search for a Chauffeur

'Corky's on the right side of right,' said Twinks as the Lagonda sped effortlessly along the road to London. 'We definitely need to recruit a top-ranker for the job.'

The chauffeur was not present to hear himself praised in this manner. It was Blotto who was at the wheel of the magnificent machine. 'And you're sure we're snuffling towards the right truffle? We'll find the right sort of boddo at this hotel, will we?'

Twinks indicated the treasury-tagged sheets on her lap. 'This is Razzy's dope. He's never wrong.'

'Good ticket,' said Blotto.

The Excelsior Hotel was in Earl's Court, a run-down part of London where one might expect penniless foreigners to foregather. Blotto parked the Lagonda directly outside the entrance and the siblings walked in. Although the people they were likely to meet did not deserve the gesture, they had put on evening dress. Even if nobody else did, the Lyminsters had standards, after all.

As they entered the ballroom, both wondered whether their mark of respect might have misfired. Though the other people present were in evening wear, their ensembles were so shabby that Blotto and Twinks's expertly tailored garments could have been designed to show them up. The assembled throng had last bought new outfits about the same time as the Bashuskys.

Indeed, stepping into that ballroom gave the impression that the Bashusky family had been somehow reduplicated into a hundred facsimiles. Men with drooping moustaches and drooping spirits stood about listlessly in patched dinner suits. The women's dresses too were darned echoes of an earlier era. Many young females gazed yearningly into the middle distance (presumably towards the unreachable Moscow). Young men sagged around, throwing back small glasses of vodka with the look of those contemplating suicide.

In a corner of the ballroom a dejected band played mournful folk tunes on triangular stringed instruments. A few couples made half-hearted moves on the dance floor.

Twinks boldly crossed to a man whose stained sash and tarnished insignia might have denoted a level of social standing in Russia under a previous regime. 'Evening, me old pineapple,' she said, hoping to put him instantly at his ease. 'We're Honoria and Devereux Lyminster. Looking for a poor old thimble who suffers under the name-tag of Count Konstantin Krupkov.'

'There is Konstantin.' Without interest the man gestured towards a thin, twitchy-looking individual who sat alone at a table with a revolver in front of him.

Blotto and Twinks crossed the floor and politely identified themselves to him. At their approach the man's eyes flashed paranoia. 'What do you want?' he demanded in a panicked voice, picking up the revolver in a panicked hand. 'Have you come here to kill me?'

'No,' Twinks replied.

'We don't look like spoffing coffinators, do we, me old toothbrush stand?' asked Blotto, endeavouring to introduce a level of casualness into the conversation.

'You never know what the Bolshevik assassins look like,' the man replied. 'They are masters of disguise as well as

42

masters of sadism. And they are everywhere!' His eyes flashed nervously around the ballroom, as though expecting hordes of Bolshevik assassins to emerge from the skirting boards.

'Well, don't don your worry-boots about us,' said Twinks. 'We're very definitely on your side. Blotto doesn't even know what a Bolshevik is.'

Her brother readily asserted that this was indeed the case. The explanations which he'd been given only a few days before by Professor Erasmus Holofernes had trickled out of his mind in precisely the same way as had the guff he was given by the beaks back at Eton. There was some filter in Blotto's brain that kept out most information and could only recall details of cricket matches and days out hunting.

Reluctantly Konstantin Krupkov put down the revolver, in a carefully chosen position on the table from which he could very easily pick it up again. 'So what is it you want?'

This being something practical, Twinks took over. 'Do you know a family called the Bashuskys?'

'I believe I have heard the name.'

'Under the Tsar they had an estate called Zoraya-Bolensk.'

Some animation came into the Count's listless visage. 'Ah yes, I do know who you mean. As it happens, the Bashuskys are distant relatives of mine.' He warmed to his theme. 'And in fact I believe they have landed on their feet since they came to England.'

'Oh, in what way?'

'Apparently they have found a bone-headed British aristocratic family to whom they are some kind of relations.' Poor ones, thought Twinks, but she didn't say anything as Konstantin Krupkov went on, 'And, because of an outdated rule of hospitality among such people, all of the Bashuskys are living with them in the lap of luxury. Well, I was thinking ... since we're relatives of the Bashuskys we must also be relatives of this English family.

So we could go and live there in the lap of luxury too! Just myself, my wife the Countess and our seventeen children. All I need is the address where the Bashuskys are so effectively milking their hosts. Since you know them, perhaps you also know the address where they are staying?'

'Absolutely no idea,' said Twinks.

'Of course you know,' said Blotto. 'Why, they're staying at—'

'*Absolutely no idea!*' Twinks repeated with considerable force.

This time Blotto got the message. 'Absolutely no idea,' he echoed, and then possibly over-egged the pudding by saying, 'I think the place they're staying is somewhere in the North of Scotland.'

'Ah well, I will do some research,' said Konstantin Krupkov. 'There cannot be so many stately homes in Great Britain.'

'Oh, actually there are millions,' said Blotto.

The Count was not so easily misled. 'But if you know the Bashuskys, you must know where they are living.'

Blotto couldn't fault the logic of that, nor could he see a way of answering that didn't involve a mention of Tawcester Towers, but fortunately his sister (not for the first time in their lives) came to his rescue. 'They are insisting that the whole thing's top-secret. Tight as a miser's mouth. You see, just like you, the Bashuskys are worried about Bolshevik assassins.'

Finally she was talking Krupkov's language. He nodded acceptance of her explanation.

'Anyway,' said Twinks, getting back to the point, 'enough of this fluff-flummery. We are involved in a secret mission with the Bashuskys.'

Again the Count's interest was kindled. 'Can you tell me what it is?'

'No,' said Twinks. 'That's why it's secret.'

'But it is a mission against the Bolsheviks?'

'Certainly is. You've won the coconut there.'

'In that case,' said Konstantin Krupkov, 'I will co-operate in any way possible. I will do anything that thwarts the evil plans of those swine. What do you need doing?'

'We need a driver who is completely trustworthy, speaks fluent Russian and is so devoted to the White Russian cause that he is prepared to risk his life for it.'

'Ah!' said the Count. 'Why did you not tell me earlier? I know exactly the man for the job.'

'Jollissimo!' said Twinks. 'Can we get to meet him?'

'Of course.' He looked cautiously around the room. 'Sometimes he is here. This evening he is not.'

'So when can we meet him?'

'You can meet him straight away. When he is not here I know where he is.'

All of Count Konstantin Krupkov's lethargy seemed to vanish as he suddenly rose from his chair, slipped the revolver into his jacket pocket and led them out of the ball-room, collecting his cloak on the way.

The evening streets of Earl's Court were ill-lit and dingy, but the Count seemed to have no doubt where he was going. Blotto and Twinks, though incredibly intrepid, were quite glad there were three of them striding through the shadows. Human shapes lurked in doorways, dogs barked, rats scuttled, and following footsteps seemed to echo their own. Blotto wished he'd brought his cricket bat with him. He always felt more secure to be armed in a sticky situation.

Their journey was not a long one. Only a few turnings away from the Excelsior Hotel Count Konstantin Krupkov stopped suddenly outside a squalid pub. Little light emanated from the grubby windows and its sign was so discoloured the name was unreadable. Krupkov ushered Blotto and Twinks inside.

It was not the kind of place where they could fade into the background. The customers who crammed the pub's dark corners all looked – and smelt – like working men.

The irruption of three people in evening dress, even though the cloak of one of them was patched and darned, could not escape attention. A communal intake of breath was followed by an unwelcoming silence.

'Well, toad-in-the-hole!' said Blotto. 'Chinny-up, everyone! It might never happen.'

His efforts at cheering up the assembled throng did not meet with total success. In fact the level of malevolence in the pub seemed to be turned up a couple of degrees.

'Dmitri Raselov!' the Count called out.

At the summons an enormous man rose out of the shadows. He was dressed in a huge black peasant smock, worn over black peasant trousers and black peasant boots. The brows on his bony forehead met to form one line of black hair. 'Yes, master,' he said to the Count.

This was a cue for the other customers to relax. If Dmitri Raselov knew the incomers, then they must be all right. The murmuring chatter they had interrupted reasserted itself.

Raselov led the three visitors across to the table from which he'd risen. Unbidden, his former drinking companions sidled away into the outer darkness, leaving seats for Blotto, Twinks and Count Krupkov. Their host sat down, but still towered over all three of them.

He took a none-too-clean cloth out of his pocket and used it to scour round the empty glasses. Then he picked up a much-handled bottle from the centre of the table and poured out four full measures.

'Vodka,' he said, 'made by my mother from only the best potatoes.'

He raised the glass to his lips. Count Krupkov, knowing the form, followed suit. Then the pair of them knocked back the contents in one and slammed the empty glasses down on the table with a cry of 'Oy!'

Blotto and Twinks, having seen what was the proper form, did exactly the same . . . well, except for the fact that

Blotto thought 'Hoopee-doopee!' fitted the occasion better than 'Oy!' Though the spirit took a few layers of skin off the interiors of their throats, they were both far too well brought up to draw attention to the fact.

'So,' said Dmitri Raselov, turning to the Count, 'what can I do for you, master?'

'I'm sorry,' said Twinks, 'but I don't quite read the semaphore here.'

'Oh?' asked Count Krupkov.

'I can't understand why Dmitri Raselov refers to you as "master". I thought all the serfs in Russia were emancipated in 1861.'

The Count smiled and spread his hands wide. 'Perhaps you would like to explain, Dmitri . . . ?'

The giant turned the full focus of his intense dark eyes on Twinks. 'Yes, the serfs were supposed to be, as you put it, "emancipated" in 1861. But not all of us agree that that was a good idea. I myself believe it is against the natural order of things. My master the Count was born into an aristocratic family, so it is right that he should rule over lesser men. I was born into a family of peasants, so it is right that I should serve my master, obeying his every command, however outlandish. And whether or not I get paid for fulfilling such services . . . well, that is up to the whim of my generous employer.' He nodded respectfully towards the Count. 'I would be happy to work with money or without money. That is how things should be. That is how things were meant to be.'

Blotto found himself spontaneously applauding. He approved strongly. When he heard what Dmitri Raselov had to say, it could have been Corky Froggett himself talking. And Blotto felt sure that his mother would have been equally pleased to hear the sentiments. The Dowager Duchess had never fully approved of the ending of the feudal system, and Blotto thought there was a lot to be said for that point of view.

47

'But, Dmitri, hold back the hounds a moment,' said Twinks. 'The Russian Revolution has turned everything on its head. The aristocrats are regarded as lumps of toad-spawn and it's the peasant classes who're now running the country. Don't you feel envious of them? Don't you want power for yourself?'

'No,' Raselov replied. 'The only power I want is the power that my master grants me. Anything Count Krupkov requires of me, he has only to say the word and it is done.'

'Well, in this particular case,' said Twinks, 'What is required is not directly *for* Count Krupkov.'

'No,' Blotto agreed, 'it's more to get us out of a glue pot.'

'This does not matter,' said Dmitri Raselov. 'If my master tells me I should do it, then do it I will.'

Blotto and Twinks looked hopefully towards Count Krupkov. With a twirl of his depleted moustaches, he announced, 'I wish that you should do as they ask, Raselov.'

'Then I will do it!' the self-appointed serf responded. 'You two I will now refer to as "master" and "mistress". What is it that you wish me to do?'

Twinks gave a brief résumé of their situation, how they were planning to return the Bashuskys to their estate at Zoraya-Bolensk. She didn't dwell on the fact that achieving this mission might well involve reversing everything that had happened since the Russian Revolution. She just explained that she and Blotto needed a driver for the Hispano-Suiza which was to accompany their Lagonda across Europe.

When she had finished, Dmitri Raselov stood up and, placing a huge hand across his massive chest, said, 'I will do what you ask. I will do it because my master Count Krupkov tells me I should do it. And I will do it also in the hope that our efforts will help restore to my homeland the proper order of society – where those who are born to rule rule over those who are born to be subservient and serve their masters!'

Blotto was once again deeply impressed by Dmitri Raselov's good sense. If more people thought like him, if more people respected the natural order of things, the world would undoubtedly be a better place.

7

# An Unexpected Problem

Having noted means of contacting Dmitri Raselov when further instructions were needed, Blotto and Twinks allowed themselves to be led back by Count Krupkov to the Excelsior Hotel. There nothing much had changed, except for the fact that more vodka had made everyone present even droopier than before. Though, as Twinks knew, British people when drinking tended to be loud and euphoric before slumping into melancholy, the White Russians seemed to skip the first part of the process and go straight down into deep depression.

Count Krupkov, aware that Blotto and Twinks would have to spend the night in London, said he felt sure there would be rooms available at the Excelsior, but they demurred at the suggestion. Instead, thanking him profusely for his help, they got into the Lagonda and Blotto drove them to the Ritz. There they booked two of the adjacent suites which the management always kept available for visiting aristocrats, and spent the rest of the evening testing the quality of the barman's latest concoctions in the cocktail bar.

The next morning Blotto felt a little the worse for wear. After trying out a few alternatives he had homed in on his favourite cocktail, a St Louis Steamhammer. This had the effect comparable to the ancient medical procedure known as trepanning, whereby a part of the skull is surgically removed to give access to the brain. After two or three St Louis Steamhammers the brain feels as if it has no protective cranium left.

As a result the following morning Blotto felt a little wan and in need of a huge restorative fry-up. So, after a breakfast which would have fed the entire population of a small town, he drove his sister back to Tawcester Towers.

'Larksissimo!' said Twinks as they emerged from grimy London suburbs on to the open road. 'Now we're really dashing away with a smoothing iron. We have our driver for the Hispano-Suiza – and he's a native Russian speaker. All of the tumblers in the lock are falling into place. The Mater will be really pleased with us, because soon it's going to be "toodle-pip, Bashuskys!"'

It was only when they got back home that they encountered a totally unexpected problem.


'I don't really wish to return to Russia,' announced Count Igor Bashusky. 'I am enjoying life here at Tawcester Towers.'

'But you keep cluntering on about it,' protested Blotto. 'All you ever talk about is getting back to your home pastures of Zoraya-Bolensk.'

'Perhaps,' the Count agreed. 'But saying one wants something is often different from knowing what one really wants.'

'But you did say that Zoraya-Bolensk was the perfect place to live,' Twinks pointed out. 'You said that the serfs on the estate simply loved working for you.'

'This was true indeed,' said the Count, and a nostalgic tear came into his eye. 'When I think how Vadim Oblonsky loved working for us . . . How to obey our every whim without question, without thought of remuneration, was the fulfilment of his most cherished dream. The same was true of his wife Galina and of their many children. They lived only to serve us.'

A dark shadow of recollection broke into his reverie. 'But that was before the vile Reds took over the reins of government. Who can say what will have happened to Zoraya-Bolensk and the Oblonskys under their cruel yoke?'

This, Twinks recognised, was dangerous talk. If the Bashuskys thought too much about what life in Russia might be like under the new regime, then the chances of ever shifting them from Tawcester Towers looked pretty slender.

They were once again in the Pink Drawing Room, awaiting the arrival of Grimshaw with the pre-prandial drinks trolley. The Dowager Duchess was not present. She continued with the lie of being 'indisposed', anything to keep her out of the company of the Russian cuckoos who had invaded her nest of Tawcester Towers.

It was a cold evening. Outside frost sparkled on the grass and trees, and the wind moaned disconsolately around the turrets of the ancestral building. Inside the Pink Drawing Room, however, there was a roaring fire. And once again, to Blotto and Twinks's mounting fury, the Bashuskys were hogging it.

Twinks turned to the Countess, remembering the strength of her melancholy nostalgia for the good old days on their estate.

'Surely,' said Twinks, 'you wish to return to Zoraya-Bolensk?'

'It is my only wish.'

This was a lot more promising than the response from the Count. Twinks had got the distinct impression during the time the Bashuskys had been in residence that the Countess was the one who wore the trousers in that particular marriage. She pressed home her advantage. 'You spoke of endless summer days when life was all creamy éclair, when you sat in the gardens of Zoraya-Bolensk drinking iced lemonade.'

'Yes, I remember them well,' agreed the Countess, the glint of a tear at the corner of her eye.

'So what we are suggesting could take you back to those scrumplicious times. You could recapture the magic you used to experience at Zoraya-Bolensk.'

The Countess sighed. 'Could we, though? I fear Zoraya-Bolensk can never again be as we remember it. Igor is right. The evil Reds will have destroyed everything.'

'Yes, but we can change all that,' said Twinks airily, hoping she wasn't about to be questioned on the details of how that aim might be achieved.

'Igor is right,' Countess Lyudmilla repeated. 'We cannot recapture what has been stolen from us forever.'

Blotto felt it was about time he made a contribution to the conversation. 'Of course you can. It's as easy as raspberries. Boddoes can recover gubbins that's been stolen from them. One of me old muffin-toasters from Eton had his cricket bat stolen from the pavilion while he was playing in the Eton and Harrow match. Well, obviously the job wasn't done by an Etonian – they're all as honest as the year is long. But there was a nasty suspicion that it might have been done by a Harrovian. They don't have quite the same code as we Etonians – and rumour has it they've even been known to admit some little 'uns without titles into the place. But it was still a bit of a social gumboil. You know, you can't go asking chaps most of whom are of your own class – or pretty damn near it – to open up their cricket bags to see if any of them contain a purloined bat. Isn't the thing.

'So my old muffin-toaster looked like he was being left with the wrong end of the sink-plunger. He'd have to give up thoughts of his cricket bat forever – and that bat had been a Grade A foundation stone for him. He'd made more centuries with it than you lot've had bottles of vodka. So he was, as you can imagine, pretty vinegared off about the whole clangdumble.

'Anyway, poor old thimble was about to reconcile himself to a bat-less – and possibly century-free – future when another of our muffin-toasters had a real buzzbanger of an idea. "Why don't we check in the groundsman's hut," he said – and I'll be jugged like a hare if that wasn't what we did. Sure enough, we found the bat the slimer had filched straight away. Huh. Just goes to show. Like in all those whodunit books some boddoes write, before you talk to the boddoes with proper breeding, first check out the oiks below stairs. Guinea to a groat you'll find your villain straight away.'

Blotto spoke these last words with a finality which implied that his case was conclusive, but the expressions on the Bashuskys' faces did not suggest they were convinced – or even if they'd understood a word he'd said.

So he spelled it out for them. 'All I'm saying is that nothing's ever lost forever. As my little story has just demonstrated.'

Count Igor Bashusky still looked puzzled. 'So you are saying that our precious estate of Zoraya-Bolensk has been stolen by the groundsman?'

'No, no, no.' Blotto paused for a moment's consideration. 'Though, on the other hand, there are distinct parallels between the two thingies. It was a four-faced filcher from the servant class who had whipawayed my muffin-toaster's cricket bat and, if I understand correctly, it's stenchers from the servant class who have whipawayed the Russian government from the Romanovs.'

Count Igor Bashusky gave a small nod of acknowledgement, but didn't seem overly impressed by what Blotto had just told him. Twinks decided it was time to move down the family hierarchy in the hope of getting support for the scheme of returning the Bashuskys to their homeland.

She turned to Sergei. 'You too have spoken of your wish to return to Russia.'

'I only wish to return to Russia,' the boy responded passionately, 'if it is in your company. So long as I am with you, Twinks, it does not matter which country I am in!'

'Well, I am planning to go with you to Russia.'

'This is good news! Then I will go to Russia. We can be married in the chapel at Zoraya-Bolensk. Our old family priest will conduct the ceremony.'

'Erm, yes.' Twinks was unwilling to give him too much hope for their relationship. Her natural honesty did not square with the idea of misleading Sergei on that subject (even though such duplicity might be a way of getting him out of Tawcester Towers). 'But then I don't want you to grab the wrong end of the pitchfork. I'm afraid, Sergei, my feelings for you haven't changed.'

'You mean you cannot love me?'

'Sorry, me old pineapple.'

'Then I will shoot myself.'

Twinks saw a potential way out. 'Couldn't you possibly wait till we get to Russia and shoot yourself there?' she suggested.

'No!' Sergei replied. 'It would be much more comfortable for me to shoot myself here than in Zoraya-Bolensk.'

Twinks didn't feel she was really getting anywhere with their mission of shifting the Bashuskys. Finally she turned to Masha, reassured that she'd be on safer ground with her. At least there was no question about the girl's keenness to return to Moscow. 'You want to travel to Russia with us, don't you, Masha?'

'I am not so sure,' the girl replied.

'But you keep saying you want to go back to Moscow!' Blotto protested. 'You keep worrying away about that like a terrier with a rat.'

'Yes,' Masha agreed. 'I do keep on saying that I want to go back to Moscow.'

'Well,' Twinks pointed out, 'now is your opportunity to realise that dream.'

'Ah yes,' said Masha, 'but maybe I am not talking in literal terms here.'

'What do you mean?'

'I think that perhaps my aspiration is metaphorical.'

'Eh?' said Blotto, completely lost.

'For me perhaps Moscow is merely a symbolic representation of adolescent yearning,' Masha continued. 'It is not the real city to which I wish to return, but an idealised version of my lost youth, for which I will be eternally in mourning.'

'Broken biscuits,' muttered Blotto. He wouldn't usually have used such an expression in mixed company, but then rarely had he been so provoked.

'I think, all in all,' Count Bashusky summed up, 'we are very happy here. And when we think back to the time we were there, we realise that Zoraya-Bolensk was in many ways rather primitive. There we did not have the electric lights and constant hot water available at Tawcester Towers. Nor did we have the access to the range of cars you have here in your garages. We travelled most of the time by droshky and sledge.'

'Also,' the Countess contributed, 'the food is better here than it was at Zoraya-Bolensk.'

'So we are much better off here,' her husband agreed.

Blotto and Twinks exchanged looks. Their plans for getting rid of the Bashuskys once and for all lay in tatters.

At that moment Grimshaw entered with the drinks trolley. As usual, their guests did not stint themselves. And the Tawcester Towers bill at the wine merchants rose once again.

Twinks realised that something had to be done. And extremely quickly.


The telephone in the ice-cold hall of Tawcester Towers was rarely used, and then mostly by the Dowager Duchess when she wished to patronise distant relatives. Use of the contraption by other family members was discouraged, but Twinks reckoned this was an emergency.

There were only two telephone lines into St Raphael's College, Oxford. One went, predictably enough, to the Porter's Lodge, where a primitive exchange system allowed calls to be redirected to the Principal, Dean of Studies or Bursar. The second led to an instrument hidden somewhere amidst the paper mountains of Professor Erasmus Holofernes's room. His international eminence as a researcher allowed him this special privilege and, though most of his enquiries were conducted by letter, there were some which could be more quickly dealt with on the telephone. Most of these were in foreign parts. As a result the telephone bill that the Professor amassed was astronomical. The fact that St Raphael's always paid it without demur was another indicator of how much they appreciated the presence of a genius in their midst.

Twinks had chosen her timing carefully. The timetable of life in an Oxford college was unvarying. Professor Erasmus Holofernes, having worked all day on his multifarious researches, would reluctantly change into his dinner suit and appear for drinks in the Senior Common Room at six-thirty. Exactly an hour (and a good few dry sherries) later he and his fellow dons would go through to the Great Hall for dinner. There they would enjoy the skills of the college chef and the carefully-selected contents of the college cellar, conversing at an intellectual level incomprehensible to lesser men and women, except for Twinks of course, had she ever been allowed to attend (which she wouldn't have been, due to her gender apart from anything else).

At the end of dinner, usually around nine-thirty, many of the dons would return to the Senior Common room to check out the college's rather fine selection of *digestifs*. Professor Erasmus Holofernes did not join them. He returned to his room, where he kept a substantial supply of the college's finest Cognac. Fortified by constant sips of this, he would continue to work late into the small hours.

For him going to bed at one o'clock constituted an early night. Frequently, however, so absorbed was he in his researches that he would still be at his desk – or at the pile of papers under which logic dictated his desk must be – when the first light of dawn showed at the leaded panes of his windows.

Twinks knew therefore that ringing him any time between nine-thirty in the evening and one in the morning she stood a good chance of getting a reply. She waited till eleven o'clock. By then the rest of her family had retired to bed, though the Bashuskys were still inflating the Tawcester Towers drinks bill in the Billiard Room.

The operator immediately connected her call to Professor Erasmus Holofernes. He was, needless to say, delighted to hear from her. His acquaintance included all of the world's finest brains, but few of them were so delightfully packaged as Honoria Lyminster.

It did not take many words for her to explain the unfortunate situation in which she and her brother found themselves. 'So, Razzy,' she concluded, a note of desperation in her cut-glass voice, 'you must have some idea how we can get out of this glue pot.'

'I will investigate the possibilities,' he replied, 'and get back to you in the morning.'

Twinks could not have asked for a better response. She had set him an impossible challenge. And there was nothing Professor Erasmus Holofernes liked better than impossible challenges.

# 8

# Holofernes Comes Up with the Goods

When he was faced by an impossible challenge, it was a point of honour with Professor Erasmus Holofernes to come up with a solution in an impossibly quick time, so Twinks was unsurprised to be summoned from her boudoir by Harvey the housemaid at ten o'clock the following morning. Nor was she surprised to hear that there was a phone call for her.

Pausing only to don one of her selection of minks to combat the chilly environment of the hall, Twinks hurried down to pick up the receiver.

It was indeed Holofernes at the other end of the line. 'I have the answer to your problem!' he announced with characteristic pride.

'Grandissimo!' responded Twinks.

'From what you told me,' the Professor went on in efficient problem-solving mode, 'your trouble stems from the fact that the Bashuskys are far too comfortable at Tawcester Towers.'

'That's it in a walnut shell,' Twinks agreed.

'So I wondered if you had considered the possibility of making them less comfortable there?'

'In what way?'

'Ensuring that the water that is brought to their bedrooms is always cold, introducing bedbugs into their beds and worms into their salads, diluting the contents of their vodka bottles with water, infiltrating—'

'Sorry, Razzy, you must rein in your roans for a moment. Though the solutions you suggest might actually bang the bull's eye, I'm afraid none of them can actually be put into practice.'

'Why ever not?'

'It's because of the Mater.'

'Oh?'

'Though she would welcome the outcome of ridding Tawcester Towers of its infestation of Bashuskys, she would regard doing the things you suggest as beyond the barbed wire.'

'Why?'

'The Lyminster family code of honour. We have a duty of hospitality to anyone staying under the roofs of Tawcester Towers. If it were to be found out in society circles – and it inevitably would be – that a member of the Lyminster family has been introducing bedbugs into the beds of our guests, it would be a scandal to match that of the Duchess of Barnstable and the bootboy.'

The Professor did not need to be reminded of this notorious case, which had transcended the bounds of the gutter press and featured in the quality dailies. No detail – even the unusual uses of the riding crop and the whipped cream – had been allowed to escape public scrutiny.

'So I'm sorry, Razzy me old jam jar, your idea's a bit of an empty revolver.'

He did not allow his obvious disappointment to show in his voice, but said airily, 'Of course I had envisaged the potential problem with you, mother, but I thought I'd run that idea by you. It wasn't my big idea, the one which I'm sure is a copper-bottomed cert to do the business.'

'So what is your big idea?' asked Twinks.

'Overnight,' said the Professor, 'I have done some research into White Russian families, particularly those who are related to the Bashuskys. Through the years there has been a lot of intermarriage between members of the Russian aristocracy. As a result there are quite a lot of blood ties to be explored.'

Twinks clapped her hands together gleefully. 'So you are saying you've found some boddoes who're more closely related to the Bashuskys than we are. People on whose grounds it would be more logical for them to pitch their tents than at Tawcester Towers?'

'No, Twinks, looking for people more closely related proved to be a blind alley. There are plenty, but none of them are in a better situation than the Bashuskys. They are all dirt poor, they have lost all the lands and possessions they owned in the old country. So they too are battening on wealthier relations. None of them are in any position to take on more hangers-on.'

'Oh.' Twinks couldn't keep her disappointment out of the monosyllable.

'But this made me think: do the Bashuskys have any relatives who are really rich, who have somehow managed to get their money out of Russia?'

'And do they?'

Twinks could instantly visualise the complacent smile on the Professor's face as he said, 'Yes, they do.'

'Who?'

'There is a family called Lewinsky who are now based in Berlin. They are aristocrats through marriage, rather looked down on by the rest of the White Russians. They do not have a long pedigree and also the business in which they are involved is not thought to be respectable.'

'So what for the love of strawberries do they do?' asked Twinks, expecting at the very least white slavery.

'They are bankers.'

'Ah.' She understood instantly. There were many professional people whose services aristocratic families had to call on from time to time, but who would never be invited to dine. Solicitors certainly fitted into that category, as did doctors and occasionally hired assassins.

But bankers were probably the least socially acceptable of the lot. Though it was by loans from them that most English country houses were kept going, the relationship was not one to which the average aristocrat would wish to draw attention. Bankers were just a rather unattractive necessity, like dustbin men and rat catchers.

Professor Erasmus Holofernes continued his explanation. 'The Lewinskys were already an international concern before the Russian Revolution. They had operations in Berlin, Paris and other European capitals. They even had a small office in New York. As a result, when the Reds took over, only the Lewinsky estates in Russia were seized. Most of their money was already out of the country.

'And during what has been a very volatile period for the banking industry – particularly in Germany – they have managed to increase their wealth exponentially. The head of the family, Pavel Lewinsky, understands the money markets like few others. Whereas many see the Great Depression as a disaster, he sees it as an opportunity. And he is making money hand over fist.

'As a result of this, he and his family live in very lavish style, with properties all over Europe. His main base is Berlin where he has a huge mansion. He could easily accommodate the Bashuskys.'

'But would he want to accommodate the Bashuskys?'

'I think that could be arranged. As I say, the Lewinskys have never quite made the grade in Russian society. A connection to a genuine aristocratic family like the Bashuskys might be just the sort of thing they would welcome.'

'But more importantly, Razzy me old banana, if the Lewinskys are such social pariahs because they're bankers, would the Bashuskys want to stay with them?'

'Listen, Twinks. From what you've told me about the Bashuskys, they're completely materialistic.'

'That's certainly the way they come across.'

'You said they want to stay at Tawcester Towers because

it's a lot more comfortable than their estate of Zoraya-Bolensk ever was.'

'You're bong on the nose there, Razzy.'

'So if it could be proved to them that the Lewinskys' mansion in Berlin is much more modern and has many more amenities than Tawcester Towers . . . well, they might think they were on a better ticket there than they are with you.'

'Yes, it could work,' said Twinks thoughtfully. 'But how are we going to convince them of the opulence in the Lewinskys' mansion?'

'That is in hand,' the Professor replied. 'I am arranging for photographs to be taken of the place inside and out. These will be posted to me by special delivery and I will organise a college messenger to take them to you at Tawcester Towers the minute they arrive.'

'And are you going to tell the Lewinskys of the invasion they are about to receive?'

'I have done that already. I sent a telegram, apparently from the Bashuskys, saying that they would shortly be in Berlin and how much they would like to meet their relatives the Lewinskys. I have had a reply, inviting the Bashuskys to stay for a weekend whenever they wish to do so.'

'That should ping the partridge,' said Twinks, recalling the Bashuskys' arrival at Tawcester Towers. 'They were only meant to be staying here for a weekend.'

'I will obviously send you copies of both sets of photographs, Twinks. And the relevant addresses for the Lewinskys. And I think,' he concluded with considerable satisfaction, 'we can confidently state that your problem is solved.'

'There's just one thing,' said Twinks.

'And what is that?'

'Well, although the Bashuskys are only foreign aristocrats – you know, not the genuine article like we are – they do still take their status very seriously. And I was just pondering ... if they do really regard the Lewinskys as below the salt, then they might feel they'd be slumming a bit to visit them, and refuse to do so.'

'I had considered that eventuality,' said the Professor smugly. 'And I have worked out the perfect solution.'

'What is that?'

'In all the paperwork you will receive the name "Lewinsky" is not mentioned once. I thought it prudent to change the name of the family whom the Bashuskys will be visiting in Berlin.'

'So what have you changed it to?'

'Romanov.'

'Grandissimo!' said Twinks. 'Give that pony a rosette!'


The minor deceit worked a treat, though Twinks had an anxious wait until she could witness its effect. She did not want to mention the proposed trip to Berlin to the Bashuskys until she was armed with all of the requisite ammunition – the photographs of the Lewinsky mansion and other documentation that Professor Erasmus Holofernes had promised. Despite all of the expense of special deliveries, they took five days to arrive, five days during which Twinks endured considerable frustration and increasingly urgent questions from her mother about when they were going to 'get rid of the stenchers!' Having set the precedent of being 'indisposed' to avoid dining with the Bashuskys, she was happy to let that situation continue, but she was also very fed up with having dinner served in her bedroom. Despite the assiduous post-prandial efforts of Harvey the housemaid with her dustpan and brush, the Dowager Duchess found she was constantly awakened by the irritation of crumbs in the sheets.

At last Twinks's wait was over. She was informed by Grimshaw that a large package had been delivered for her, and she found within everything that Professor Erasmus Holofernes had promised.

She presented the documentation to the Bashuskys in the Pink Drawing Room at drinks before dinner that evening, and was delighted with the reception that it elicited. The Count and Countess were impressed by the opulence of the Lewinskys' mansion, agreeing that it demonstrated a level of luxury that Tawcester Towers could not begin to match.

Blotto was rather annoyed at the way their unwanted guests disparaged his home, but a warning look from Twinks's azure eyes persuaded him to keep his feelings to himself.

What really swung it for the Bashuskys, however, was not just the upgrade in accommodation offered in Berlin, but the name on the telegram (suitably doctored by Holofernes) which invited them to stay. Romanov. There was a great deal of snobbery amongst the White Russians and any contact with relations of the former ruling family was highly valued.

There was one further wrinkle in the Professor's plan which he had deliberately omitted to tell Twinks. To ensure a warm welcome in Berlin for the émigrés from Tawcester Towers, he had also in all correspondence with the Lewinskys changed the surname of the Lyminsters' unwanted guests to 'Romanov'. But he did say that 'for security reasons' they would be travelling under the name 'Bashusky'.

# 9

# An Intruder in the Boudoir

After dinner that night Blotto joined Twinks in her boudoir for a cup of cocoa, and the mood between them was extremely jolly. As usual, Twinks made the cocoa herself without any help from below stairs, heating the water up in an electric kettle and adding the powder, milk and sugar as if it were the kind of thing she did every day. Blotto was frequently awestruck by what a modern woman his sister was.

'Well, hoopee-doopee!' he said when she passed him his cup. 'What a biffing stick that Professor of yours is, eh, Twinks me old boot-brush! All we have to do is deliver the spoffing Bashuskys to Berlin and we'll be rolling on camomile lawns!'

'Yes, it is rather terrifulous, Blotto me old shaving bowl,' Twinks agreed. 'They seem to have swallowed the idea, hook, line and wodjermabit. Good old Razzy!'

'He really is the panda's panties.' In Blotto's lexicon there was no higher praise.

'The Mater'll be pleased as Punch when she hears the glad tidings. I don't know how much longer she could have survived spending every evening confined to quarters.'

'So when do you reckon we'll get under starter's orders for the Berlin steeplechase?'

'Soon as we possibly can. Shouldn't take long for the staff to pack the Bashuskys' stuff – they hardly own anything. Then we'll have to contact Dmitri Raselov, but that shouldn't be too tough a rusk to chew. Get on to Count Krupkov and Raselov will jump to do anything his master asks him to. No, I reckon we can be away by the weekend.'

'And how long do you reckon the whole clangdumble will take?'

'Inside a week, Blotto, no probs. This particular shooting match is going to be a lot easier now we're only going to Berlin. Getting to Russia and reversing the effects of the Russian Revolution might have kept us away from our snug little Tawcester Towers beds for quite a while, but the situation has suddenly become as easy as a country barmaid. No, I can't see that we're likely to encounter any problemettes. What do you reckon, Blotters?'

'Only one potential chock in the cogwheel so far as I can see, Twinks me old butter pat, is Corky Froggett.'

'Oh?'

'Well, it's going to be a bit of a poser for him to be in Berlin, surrounded by sausage-munchers and not being allowed to shoot any of them.'

'But surely, if we explain to him the reasons why he can't?'

'Oh yes, he'll take it like a trooper, don't don your worry-boots about that. He just may feel a little uncomfortable, that's all.'

'Tell him it's in a good cause. And tell him he'll be maintaining the honour of the Lyminsters.'

'That's the right ticket, yes.'

'Well, Blotters, I must say I feel in zing-zing condition.'

'Me too.'

'Having got to this point, nothing can go wrong,' said Twinks triumphantly, little realising how horribly inaccurate her assessment would prove to be.


The behaviour of the Bashuskys during the remainder of their stay at Tawcester Towers provided evidence of the fact that good breeding is not always an indicator of good manners. Now that they had seen the photographed splendours of the Lewinskys' – or, as far as they were concerned the Romanovs' – lifestyle in Berlin, all they seemed able to do was to disparage their current accommodation.

Whereas their previous model for comparison had been the somewhat primitive amenities of Zoraya-Bolensk, they were now all too aware of the inadequacies of the Tawcester Towers' arrangements. They complained of the draughts and the fact that the fire in the Pink Drawing Room didn't give out enough heat (rich, thought Blotto and Twinks, coming from the people who actually prevented its heat from reaching the rest of the room). The Tawcester Towers' plumbing, which the Bashuskys had formerly praised, was a source of complaint now they had seen pictures of the magnificent bathrooms owned by the Lewinsky/Romanovs. They even started to grumble about the quality of the vodka that Grimshaw served to them in such quantities.

Blotto was very incensed by these criticisms of the earthly paradise that Tawcester Towers represented for him, and was tempted to take the Bashuskys to task about their comments. But his sister restrained him, pointing out that all of their guests' carping made it clear that they had absolutely no intention of returning to Tawcester Towers in any circumstances. Blotto had only to keep his temper for a few days and then their stately home would be Bashusky-free forever.

Meanwhile Dmitri Raselov had been contacted and stood in readiness to drive the Hispano-Suiza to Berlin as soon as he got the word. Corky Froggett did more fine-tuning of the Lagonda's monster of an engine. Twinks's maid and Blotto's valet started to pack the clothes their betters would require during their extended sojourn in Europe. The domestics could be trusted to perform this task without supervision, but for each of the siblings there was one item which they would look after themselves. For

Twinks it was her sequinned reticule, whose contents had frequently proved invaluable in tight spots. And for Blotto it was his cricket bat.

Over the previous days Twinks had made other preparations for foreign travel. She had collected road maps for most of Europe to take with her. She also studied and memorised the street map of Berlin. She liked to know her way around any unfamiliar city.

The maps were put in her reticule, along with a lot of other equipment which had proved invaluable to the success of previous adventures she and her brother had undertaken.

Twinks went through her mental checklist of preparations. She had made provisional reservations of suites for herself and Blotto at the Hotel Adlon in Berlin. She also organised an account for herself at Berlin's biggest department store, the KaDeWe (short for Kaufhaus des Westens). Just in case she needed to do any shopping. Twinks always planned ahead.

The Dowager Duchess meanwhile did not stir from her bedroom, but stayed there in a state of suspended animation. For her life would only begin again once the last Bashusky had shaken the dust of Tawcester Towers off their heels.

One of the nights before their departure to foreign climes Twinks had a shock. She was in her boudoir preparing for bed when she noticed that one of her wardrobe doors stood slightly ajar. This was an uncharacteristic oversight on the part of her housemaid. But as Twinks crossed the room to close the door she was aware of movement from inside the wardrobe. She opened it wide to reveal the defiant figure of Sergei Bashusky. In one hand he held a revolver.

'Great galumphing goatherds!' cried Twinks. 'Have you come here to shoot me?'

'No,' the boy replied. 'I have come here to shoot myself!'

'Well, that's not very thoughtful. My boudoir is a very pretty room and if you shot yourself here you'd make a real mish-mash of a mess.'

'I do not care about that,' said Sergei. 'The serfs can clear it up.'

'That's all very well, but I don't think you should be shooting yourself anyway. In polite society that kind of thing – particularly if done in a lady's boudoir – is considered a bit beyond the barbed wire.'

'I do not care about the usages of polite society. A free spirit like mine cannot be bound by such petty restrictions. Anyway, I have told you before I am going to shoot myself. And you know the reason why.'

'Is it still because you're madly in love with me?' asked Twinks, just playing for time. She knew the likely answer.

And she got it. 'Of course that is why I have to shoot myself. My love for you is so great that even to contemplate life without you is too painful for me to accept. I will be better off dead.'

'Well, that is a point of view.' For a moment Twinks was tempted. To let Sergei have his head in this matter would immediately reduce the Bashusky problem by a quarter. On the other hand, a suicide at Tawcester Towers might not be quite the thing. There hadn't been one there since the death of the sixth Duke, 'Rupert the Fiend'. And even that wasn't completely clear-cut. There had been strong rumours at the time that the poison which killed him had actually been administered by his Chinese mistress.

The other strong argument against just allowing Sergei Bashusky to shoot himself was the potential reaction of the Dowager Duchess. She might have seen such an event as a rather lax interpretation of duty of care which must be afforded to all guests to Tawcester Towers (even infuriating ones like the Bashuskys). No, Twinks rather reluctantly convinced herself, she would have to try to talk the young man out of his suicidal intentions.

'Look,' she said, 'why don't you come out of that wardrobe so that we can have a proper chat? I could rustle up a cup of cocoa for you if you like . . . ?'

'Cocoa is a drink for children,' said Sergei as he emerged from the wardrobe. 'I am not a child, I am a man. I should drink not cocoa, but vodka.'

'Well, that's all tiddle and pom,' said Twinks, 'but the fact remains that I don't have any vodka up here but I do have cocoa. I'm going to have a cup. Why don't you join me?'

Grudgingly, Sergei Bashusky conceded that he would have a cup.

'And do sit down. I can't have you standing there like a spare mule at a donkeys' ding-dong.'

Again grudgingly, Sergei Bashusky deposited himself on one of Twinks's chaises longues. She chattered to him while she made the cocoa.

'The fact is,' she said, 'I'm really flattered by what you say about me. I'm as pleased as a spaniel with two sausages. But I do think we have to be a teedly bit realistic.'

'Realism,' said Sergei mournfully, 'is the last resort of the unimaginative. To dream is better. And to have your dreams come true is the best of all.'

'So your particular dream, in relation to me, is that we should get married – is that right?'

'If that happened, I would be in heaven.'

'Yes, but where would I be?' Twinks asked, reasonably enough.

'You would be in heaven too. I would ensure that you had everything that you wished for.'

'Just as a matter of interest . . . how would you ensure that?'

'What do you mean?'

'Well, I'm afraid, to be brutally practical about the situation, getting married and all that rombooley requires a lot of the old jingle-jangle. You can't get married for nothing, particularly if you are brought up in a family like mine.

71

However you square the triangle, it's going to cost acres of spondulicks. And I can't help observing that your family seems to have a marked lack of spare crinkly stuff.'

'This will not be a problem,' said Sergei airily.

'Why not?'

'If you agree to marry me, then I will become part of the Lyminster family. Your mother, the Dowager Duchess, will find money to pay for everything. And when we are man and wife obviously my family will be able to stay here at Tawcester Towers for as long as they wish.'

As if Twinks had not already got enough strong arguments against the idea of marrying Sergei Bashusky, he had just presented her with an enormous one. Handing his cocoa across to him, she tried a different tack. 'There's another thing we have to consider in any discussion about you and me getting married, Sergei, and that is the question of age.'

'I do not care how old you are!' he cried with more passion than gallantry.

'No, that is not exactly what I meant. I mean that you are still a boy. You are not old enough to take on the adult responsibilities of marriage.'

'Very well,' he said. 'We will not get married!'

Twinks felt a huge sense of relief. She had not expected him to be persuaded so easily by her arguments.

'No,' Sergei went on. 'We will just have an affair.'

'Ah.' This was not what she had been hoping to hear.

But the boy was very enthused by the idea. 'Yes, it will be good! An affair with an older woman initiating a young boy into the secrets of love. You will be my teacher.'

Don't count your blue tits before they're born, thought Twinks, not particularly relishing the role for which Sergei was casting her in his latest fantasy.

'It will be very perfect,' he went on. 'Losing my virginity is a matter of enormous importance. Had we stayed in Russia of course my father would have completed my sentimental education by taking me to an experienced woman in one of the brothels of Moscow, but sadly that cannot happen now. But having a *grande affaire* with you will serve exactly the same purpose.'

Twinks liked the part she was being given even less.

Sergei Bashusky clapped his hands with glee. 'Yes, an affair is the answer. It will be better perhaps that our passion is not bridled by the bourgeois conformities of marriage. What we share transcends such restrictions.'

'Actually, Sergei me old cufflink, hate to be literal, but there isn't anything we share ... except for cocoa made from the same kettle.'

'But we share love!'

'No, Sergei, this is where my point doesn't seem to be being pinned to the canvas. All the love you so charmingly refer to is on your side. Maybe you do feel love for me. Maybe you are at the mercy of tempestuous passions. But I feel absolutely nothing for you. Rather less than nothing, actually. In fact, the strongest feeling I have towards you is one of considerable irritation.'

'But you don't think your attitude towards me might change when we are in the middle of a torrid affair?'

'There's about as much chance of that happening as there is of the Venus de Milo clapping.'

'You mean there is no chance?'

'Not the tidgiest gnat's breath of a chance.'

Sergei Bashusky raised the revolver barrel to his temple. 'Then I will shoot myself,' he announced.

'No, don't do that,' said Twinks wearily, and she was relieved to see him lower the gun. 'Listen, Sergei, you're very young, you have great dollops of life ahead of you, and the world is full of beautiful women for you to fall in love with.'

'But none of them is as beautiful as you are, Twinks.'

She knew that this was probably true, but to acknowledge the fact at that moment would only weaken her argument, so she went on, 'And amongst all those beautiful women I am sure there will be one whose feelings for you are as strong as the feelings that you currently feel.'

She wasn't sure how much she believed the words she was saying. It was hard to imagine any woman falling for the pimply youth currently perched on a chaise longue in her boudoir.

'Yes,' he protested, 'but whoever this woman may be, she will not be you.'

'That is the point I'm making, Sergei. The woman who is the right one for you is not me. It is not anyone whom you have yet met. All that lies ahead in your life.'

'But the woman will not be you?'

'No, it will not be me,' said Twinks, glad that he finally seemed to be taking the point on board.

Once again the mouth of his revolver was pressed into the flesh of his temple. 'Then if I have no hope of ever having any hope with you, I will shoot myself.'

'Why, suddenly?' asked Twinks. 'Nothing has changed in the tidgiest degree since you arrived here. You told me as soon as you met me that you had fallen in love with me. I made it as clear as an elephant in a railway carriage that I didn't feel the same about you. You threatened suicide then.

'Since that time, I am glad to say, though you have talked about it to the point of tedium, you have as yet not shot yourself. So why suddenly now are you getting keen on the idea again?'

'Because we are about to part. You and I. Forever!'

'What the Great Wilberforce are you talking about?'

'My parents have told me we are leaving Tawcester Towers in a couple of days and going to Berlin.'

'Yes.'

'So I will never see you again. You will not be in Berlin.'

'But I will. Blotto and I are also going to Berlin.'

Sergei Bashusky's face was immediately infused with a shade of ecstasy. 'You will be going to Berlin! In Berlin we can start our *grande affaire*. In Berlin we can be together forever!'

Twinks was just too tired to put the boy right once again. She was just glad that the prospect of his seeing her in Berlin had been sufficient to make him remove the gun from his temple and, after more tedious protestations of his love for her, leave the boudoir and let her get to bed.

But she knew all she had achieved was a stay of execution.

# 10

# Relief for the Dowager Duchess

'Good riddance to bad rubbish,' said the Dowager Duchess as she and the current Duke of Tawcester watched the convoy of Lagonda and Hispano-Suiza make its way down the long drive to the gates of Tawcester Towers.

They were in the Grey Dining Room which commanded an extensive view over the front of the estate. Smaller than the house's other dining rooms, and so rarely used for entertaining guests, it was nonetheless ideal for intimate family meals. Or it would have been had not the concept of 'intimate family anything' been so alien to the Lyminsters.

The departure that the Dowager Duchess was celebrating that morning seemed to have been infinitely delayed. Twinks had dictated that the Berlin party should leave at seven o'clock. As a result Corky Froggett and Dmitri Raselov had had the Lagonda and the Hispano-Suiza tuned up and ready on the gravel in front of Tawcester Towers at six-thirty. Blotto had got up at what to him seemed a ridiculously early hour so that he could say an appropriately sentimental farewell to Mephistopheles. Then he and Twinks had been ready to leave at the appointed time, but they hadn't taken into account the congenital lethargy of the Bashusky family.

Packing for them should have been simple. Basically everything they had brought to Tawcester Towers should leave with them. The entire Lyminster family had no wish to be reminded of their existence by any tiny item left behind. And the Tawcester Towers domestic staff were more than ready to fill their trunks and valises for them.

But the Bashuskys dithered. They dithered about how everything should be packed, into which bag every item should be bestowed. They dithered about which of their possessions should be accessible for the inevitable nights in European hostelries which would punctuate their journey to Berlin. They dithered about everything.

This wasn't helped by the fact that Blotto and Twinks had allowed the Bashuskys access to their wardrobes to pick through any cast-off garments that might fit them. Now the Russian guests were leaving, the Lyminsters could not see any reason why they should not be allowed to look a little less shabby. It was important that they should appear vaguely respectable when they met the Lewinskys in Berlin. But allowing the Bashuskys the run of Blotto and Twinks's wardrobes just gave them more decisions to dither about.

They also, perhaps encouraged by this largesse, like uncouth guests in a hotel helped themselves to quite a lot of the Lyminsters' other personal property – and had the nerve to ask the Tawcester Towers staff to pack the objects they'd purloined. This was perhaps acceptable when all they were taking were towels and pillow cases, but when they started adding brass candlesticks and silver statuettes to their haul, Grimshaw the butler, alerted to what was going on by Harvey the housemaid, decided he should have a word with the Dowager Duchess.

To his surprise all she said was, 'Let them take whatever they want – except for the portraits in the Long Gallery. Anything so long as they leave!' That was a measure of how exasperated she had become with her unwanted guests.

As a result of all these delays it was after half past twelve when the Lagonda and the Hispano-Suiza were ready to depart. There had been another moment of potential interruption when Count Igor Bashusky, looking at his watch, announced that perhaps they should stay for lunch. But an exasperated Twinks soon put a stop to that idea, informing him that hampers of cold meats and even colder champagne had been stowed in the dickies of both cars.

The Dowager Duchess did not see her guests off. Having managed to avoid any encounter with a Bashusky for the past week, she decided to maintain the illusion of being 'indisposed' for a little longer. She just watched their final departure with glee from the Grey Dining Room.

A lavish lunch had been ordered for her and the Duke. Turtle soup followed by pheasant with all the trimmings. The Tawcester Towers cellars had been explored by Grimshaw to yield up an excellent 1895 Perrier Jouet champagne and a bottle of 1873 Château Margaux.

The Dowager Duchess rejoiced in the first meal she had eaten outside her bedroom for a week.

She rejoiced less in the fact that she was sharing it with her elder son. He was, after all, the one who had invited the Bashuskys into their home in the first place.

The Duke of Tawcester – universally known as Loofah – had not been born with the intellectual acuity of his sister. When it came to brainpower the lottery of genetics had created something closer to Blotto. Indeed, an interesting academic study could be pursued into which of the two brothers was the stupider.

Loofah's real first name was Rupert. Like so many things in his life, this was something over which he had no control. All male firstborns in the Lyminster family were called Rupert, just as all second sons of the dynasty were called Devereux.

Rupert Lyminster had known from birth what his destiny was to be. The minute his father popped his clogs, he, Loofah, would become Duke of Tawcester. No two ways about it.

The change of status, he had recognised at the time, would not lead to any change in the casual proceedings of his life. He could of course now make appearances in the House of Lords, though it was an option he rarely took up. He always went along on the day when a particularly good Christmas Lunch was served to the assembled peers, but that was about it.

As to the running of the estate and general decision-making, he did not flutter the dovecotes by making any changes there. All of that side of things was still done by the Dowager Duchess. Just as it had been while his father was alive.

So Loofah was always at a bit of a loose end at Tawcester Towers. When he was there he did a lot of shooting, which he quite enjoyed, the measure of a day's success still being the number of avian corpses gathered together by the retrievers.

He also spent quite a lot of time in London's Mayfair where he had a house. When he was there he had long lunches and dinners at various clubs, where he brayed inconsequential observations to fellow aristocrats, who brayed back inconsequential responses.

Also when in London he sometimes paid for the pleasure of female company, particularly that of one large and accommodating woman who didn't care whether there was even a vestige of brain left in his cranium. She mothered him, an experience which he had never encountered during the hands-off upbringing the Dowager Duchess had bestowed with magnanimous fairness on all of her offspring.

By the ruses of being out shooting all day when he was at Tawcester Towers and otherwise being in London, Loofah managed most of the time to avoid the major responsibility of his life. This concerned his wife, who before marriage had had a portfolio of titles to match his own, but was universally known around Tawcester Towers as 'Sloggo'.

She was a woman of unprepossessing angularity and the duty that Loofah had towards her, the thing everyone in the Lyminster family expected of him, was to produce a male heir. Many attempts had already been made to achieve this happy outcome, but so far without success. A parade of small girls, all bearing a painful resemblance to their mother, appeared with monotonous regularity in the Tawcester Towers nurseries. Obviously they were sent off as soon as possible (round the age of five) to board at convents (though the Lyminsters disliked everything about the Rock Cake religion, they did approve of the faith's repressive approach to education). But there still always seemed to be far too many small girls in evidence round the place.

So Loofah had grimly to continue with his task of trying to impregnate Sloggo with a boy. It was his duty as a member of the Lyminster dynasty. The line must be continued. If all of his efforts failed, the ghastly prospect loomed of Blotto inheriting the title (a fate which Blotto himself was as appalled by as were the rest of his family). It was a very long time since a Duke of Tawcester had not been called Rupert. (The case in question had been in the sixteenth century when Duke Rupert the Apoplectic had died of apoplexy, thus passing the title to his younger brother Duke Devereux the Clumsy who had fortunately managed to produce a male heir, inevitably called Rupert, before falling, with fatal consequences, into a vat of mulled wine.)

But at least, lunching with his mother in the Grey Dining Room after watching the Bashuskys leave Tawcester Towers, he wasn't suffering from the Dowager Duchess's usual complaints about the lack of a male heir. She was still far too preoccupied by the shortcomings of her Russian visitors.

'Poor relations!' she fumed. 'Whoever invented poor relations should be shot.'

'Might not work, Mater,' suggested Loofah.

'Hm?'

'Whoever invented poor relations. Probably God. Difficult to shoot.' People who knew Loofah well got used to his manner of speaking in short sentences, rather like blasts from a shotgun, leaving time to reload.

'What are you talking about, Loofah?'

'God. Supposed to sit on a cloud. In heaven. Difficult to get a decent shot at Him.'

'Why do you talk such a lot of nonsense, Loofah?'

'Heredity?' he hazarded. 'The Pater. Talked a lot of nonsense. Didn't he?'

The Dowager Duchess thought back on her married life. The late Duke and she had endeavoured to spend as little time in each other's company as possible but when she came to think about it, she had to concede that he had talked a lot of nonsense.

'So where? Blotto and Twinks. Where're they going?'

'So long as they return without the wretched Bashuskys, I neither know nor care.'

'Some talk. I heard. Going to Berlin.' His mother shrugged. 'Twinks talked of Russia.'

This appeared to interest the Dowager Duchess no more than his previous suggestion.

'Dangerous place. Russia,' Loofah said.

'So I believe.'

'Dangerous for our sort. Country's been taken over by peasants.'

The Dowager Duchess shuddered. 'How revolting.'

'If the Bashuskys get to Russia. Won't stand a chance.'

'That is not my problem,' said the Dowager Duchess serenely.

'If Blotto and Twinks go with the Bashuskys. Not good for them either.'

'Well, that's their look-out,' said his mother. The Dowager Duchess's rather narrow range of emotions had never encompassed sentimentality about her children.

'So you won't worry, Mater? If neither of them come back?'

81

'Well ...' She thought for a moment. 'Be a pity to lose Twinks. I still have hopes of breeding from her ... you know, given the right husband, who I'm sure must be lurking somewhere in the shallows of *Burke's Peerage*.'

'And Blotto?'

'Blotto should be able to look after himself.'

'And if he can't?'

'Then he can't.' The Dowager Duchess shrugged again.

The Duke of Tawcester felt rather threatened by this apparent callousness from his parent. 'Would you feel the same, Mater? If I was the one? Risking my life in Russia?'

'No, of course not.' Loofah beamed with relief. 'Totally different situation with you. You're the Duke. Blotto's only a younger son.'

'But I thought. Conventional wisdom. Aristocratic families. Need an heir and a spare. You'd need Blotto. If something happened to me.'

'But nothing is going to happen to you,' said the Dowager Duchess. 'At least not before that wife of yours produces a male heir. How's that going, by the way?'

'Only girls,' Loofah replied mournfully.

'And is Sloggo pregnant at the moment?'

'No, she isn't.'

'Then what the hell are you doing lingering over lunch, Loofah?' the Dowager Duchess demanded. 'You should be with Sloggo, trying. And then trying again. You know what your duty is, don't you, Loofah?'

'Yes,' said the Duke of Tawcester miserably, and he left the Grey Dining Room to go and find his wife.

The journey of the Lagonda and the Hispano-Suiza from Tawcester Towers to Berlin was uneventful, though there were details about it which annoyed Blotto and Twinks. Most of these were caused by the general languor of the Bashuskys. Their late start on the day of departure meant that the convoy of two cars arrived at Dover too late for the last ferry, so they had to book into a hotel. And, need-less to say, there was not a murmur about the Bashuskys contributing to the bill for their accommodation – or for the extremely lavish dinner they ordered.

Similar problems arose on their journey through Northern Europe. Blotto and Corky Froggett had done their calculations and reckoned they could get from Dover to Berlin in two long days of driving, but the dilatoriness of the Bashuskys meant more late starts and the necessity of two nights in hotels rather than one. Again the Lyminsters footed the bill.

And when the party arrived at the Hotel Adlon where Twinks had booked suites for herself and Blotto, it was too late in the evening for the Bashuskys to contact the Lewinskys (or as they thought Romanovs) until the fol-lowing morning. Which meant very expensive rooms – and dinner – being booked for them too.

The delayed journey also meant that the Tawcester Towers party had arrived on the Saturday evening rather than the Friday midday as intended, so the weekend the Bashuskys were supposed to be spending with the Lewinsky/Romanovs was already considerably curtailed. But the following morning Twinks quickly overruled Count Bashusky's suggestion that they should stay at the Hotel Adlon till the following Friday and start their week-end then.

Firmly she announced that she would telephone the Lewinsky/Romanovs from one of the booths in the hotel lobby that very morning. Her call to the Lewinsky mansion was put through a series of underlings until she finally reached Pavel Lewinsky. In fluent German (Twinks was fluent in most European languages, as well as a few oriental ones) she announced that his weekend guests had arrived from England.

'Ah yes, of course,' he said (in German of course). 'The Romanovs.'

'The actual name-tag of these particular boddoes is Bashusky,' said Twinks (in fluent German slang).

'Of course it is, how silly of me to get it wrong,' said Pavel Lewinsky, in a voice that suggested he was tapping his nose in complicity as he spoke.

He said he would send a car to pick up the Bashuskys from the Adlon.

Back in the hotel lobby Twinks broke the glad tidings to her brother. They were both ecstatic with relief. Finally they would be seeing the back of the horracious Bashuskys.

# 11

# The Dashing Cossack

Needless to say, there was more delay before the Bashuskys actually left. Transferring their luggage from the Hispano-Suiza to the Lewinsky/Romanov Mercedes-Benz limousine took far longer than it need have done, with Countess Lyudmilla fussing over every detail.

Their departure was also delayed by Sergei insisting on having a long farewell to Twinks. He assured her that he would come to find her again at the Adlon as soon as his family had been settled into the (as he thought it) Romanovs' mansion. Twinks assured him that she would be there waiting for him (though that was the last thing she intended to be). Sergei assured her that if he did not find her again, he would shoot himself. Twinks had by then so much lost compassion for the boy that she didn't care if he did. She just hoped he wouldn't do it somewhere that made too much of a mess.

Eventually Blotto and Twinks found themselves standing outside the Adlon (address: 1 Unter den Linden) waving goodbye to the departing limousine. It was a brisk but beautiful winter's day. The weather had got colder the further East they went. The windscreens of parked cars were occluded with frost, and the heavy dark clouds suggested the imminence of snow. Blotto and Twinks gazed up to the towering beauty of the Brandenburg Gate before looking at each other and bursting into spontaneous grins.

They went to the Hotel Adlon's magnificent coffee house for a celebratory drink. Because it was only just after breakfast Blotto continued with more of the hotel's excellent coffee while his sister drank hot chocolate.

She raised her cup in a mock-toast. 'Well, larksissimo, Blotters!' she cried. 'We're finally free of that load of toadspawn. Give rosettes to both the ponies!'

'Hoopee-doopee!' Blotto agreed. 'And now there's nothing to stop us zapping straight back to Tawcester Towers.'

'Blotters,' said his sister, 'we're in one of the greatest cities of the world. Don't you think we should spend some time sightseeing?'

'No,' said Blotto. The only sights he wanted to see were all at Tawcester Towers. 'No, we want to head back home, to receive the blessings of a grateful Mater.'

'Maybe,' said Twinks. For someone of her intellect, missing out on a cultural tour of Berlin was a more serious issue. Then she added cautiously, 'Of course the Mater never does say thank you, does she? Not for anything.'

'Well, no. But I can always tell when she's pleased by something I've done.'

'Oh? How's that?'

'Well, Twinks me old slice of seed cake, I remember once when I was in the nursery and something very unusual happened.'

'What was that?'

'The Mater actually came in.'

'Came into the nursery?' asked Twinks, aghast at the idea.

'Yes.'

'Well, I'll be jugged like a hare!'

'Yes, I was pretty wobbled, I can tell you, Twinks. She'd never done anything like that before.' It was true. The

86

Dowager Duchess's aim in parenthood had always been to see as little of her offspring as was humanly possible.

Blotto went on, 'And the Mater said she'd heard from below stairs that I'd been following the shooting party that day.'

'And had you?'

'Oh yes.'

'And how old would you have been?'

'About five, I suppose.'

Twinks was impressed. 'Good ticket, Blotters,' she murmured.

'Anyway, the Mater had heard that one of the guests on the shoot – boddo was a minor member of the Royal Family as it happens – anyway, wasn't as hot on accuracy as he might have been and he'd managed to pepper one of the retrievers. Poor little beast was badly injured, so I'd done the decent thing and strangled it, you know, to put it out of its misery. And the Mater was very impressed when she heard about that.'

'So she should have been.'

'Anyway, that's why she'd come into the nursery, to say that she was impressed with what I'd done.'

'And did she give you any reward, Blotters?'

'In a way, yes.'

'What was it?'

'She told the Nanny only to give me nine spanks on the BTM with the back of the hairbrush, rather than the usual ten.'

'Crikey-mikey!' said Twinks, again deeply impressed.

'So you see,' Blotto summed up, 'I can always read the semaphore when the Mater's pleased with something I've done.'

Twinks might have questioned her brother further about quite how he was going to apply this measure of his mother's geniality to their current situation, had she not been interrupted by the approach of a dashing man in a rather Ruritanian military uniform. It was not unlike the one that Count Igor Bashusky had worn, though not at all shabby. Black knee-length boots, tight white trousers and a blue jacket with shining curlicues of gold frogging. A sheathed sabre hung from his belt. He had long wavy brown hair and a magnificent outcrop of moustaches.

'Zounds!' he cried. 'I have found that which for all of my life I have been seeking!'

'Sorry?' said Blotto. 'Not on the same page.'

But it was not to Blotto that the newcomer's words had been addressed. In fact Blotto should have expected that. He quickly recognised the symptoms. The man's face had that pallor and pop-eyed look of a boiled fish which Blotto had seen so often on those encountering his sister for the first time.

The soldier's next words confirmed Blotto's diagnosis of the situation. 'I may have deluded myself that I have experienced love before, but now I know that I have only been paddling in the shallows of infatuation. Now that I see your perfect face I know that my quest for fulfilment is ended.'

Blotto had heard this kind of guff a good few times before, and normally Twinks was pretty resistant to it. But on this occasion there was a disturbingly soupy look in her eyes as she said, 'I'm sorry, sir, but I haven't a bat's squeak of an idea whom I have the honour of addressing.'

'Nor do I know your name,' said the romantic hero. 'All I know is that my love for you flows with the force of the greatest waterfall in the world. It is a love so powerful that it sweeps before it all obstacles that might lie in its path.'

Man and woman gazed at each other with mutual soupi-ness. Blotto, experienced in seeing boddoes fall for his sister like noosed-up murderers through trap doors, thought he ought to bring a bit of sanity into the proceedings.

'Listen, me old pineapple, the lady you're addressing is only my sis, Honoria Lyminster, known to all and the rest as Twinks. Now maybe if you can share with us what it says on your name-tag, we might be able to pongle on with a bit of normal conversation.'

'I,' said the military man, 'am Count Kasimir Petrovsky and I am a Cossack.'

'Cossack?' Blotto wasn't sure that he'd heard the word before. 'Oh, in church. You mean like one of those things vicars wear?'

'No,' said Twinks.

'Oh, then is it the thing you kneel on?'

'No,' said Twinks. Blotto was unsurprised when his sister then went into a short potted history. He was used to her having such information at her fingertips. 'The Cossacks,' she said, 'are a warlike East Slavic people originating from the Ukraine and Southern Russia. After internal conflicts with the Russian Empire, by the end of the eighteenth century the Cossack nations were formed into a *Sosloviye* or "military class". Their forces played a significant role in Russia's wars, such as the Great Northern War, The Seven Years' War, The Napoleonic Wars and many others. The Cossacks have always been renowned throughout the known world and the unknown bits for their bravery and gallantry.'

'This is true,' Count Kasimir Petrovsky agreed. 'We are also the world's greatest lovers.'

'Toad-in-the-hole!' said Blotto. Some distant recollection from somewhere came to him through the fogs of memory. 'Are you the boddoes who dance sitting down?'

'The Cossacks are very great dancers, this is certainly true.' He looked puzzled. 'Though I am not sure that we can be said to dance sitting down.'

'One thing . . .' said Twinks, her azure eyes still locked on Petrovsky's brown ones. 'How did you know to address us in English?'

The Russian pointed to Blotto and let out a hearty chuckle. And when Twinks looked around the coffee house, she could see his point. There was no one else there dressed in the kind of ancestral tweeds, highly polished brogues and Old Etonian tie that her brother was sporting.

'But I do not wish to be distracted by such details,' Petrovsky went on. 'They are irrelevant at this, the most magical moment of my life, when for the first time I meet the woman I am destined to love for the rest of my days.'

Twinks would not normally have been affected by such words. She had heard similar declarations so many times from so many amorous swains that they were rather like water off a duck's back for her. But she could not deny that Count Kasimir Petrovsky was an extremely attractive man.

'One other question I must ping at you . . .' she said, 'is how you come to speak such excellent English?'

'I learned it from reading English romantic novels.'

Well, that makes sense, thought Twinks.

'One thing I must ask *you*,' said Petrovsky, 'is how on this fine Sunday morning you come to be in the coffee house of the Hotel Adlon in Berlin?'

'Ah. Well, we have some distant relatives who are White Russians called—'

The Count raised a white-gloved finger to his mustachioed lips. 'I must stop you,' he said in an urgent whisper. 'It is very risky here in Berlin to talk of such things. There are Bolshevik spies everywhere.' He looked nervously around the opulent coffee house. 'Some of the waiters here will be Bolshevik spies. If we are to talk of such things we must not do it here.'

'Does this mean,' said Blotto, his brain slowly making the connection, 'that you are a White R—?'

'Ssh!' said the Count ferociously. 'As I said, we cannot talk of such things here.'

'Then where can we gab about them?' asked Twinks.

'Meet me tonight,' replied Petrovsky, 'at the Zammer Kabaret on Winkelstrasse. Nine o'clock. There we can talk in safety.'

'Ah, sorry, we can't do that,' apologised Blotto. 'We'll be on our way back to Blighty by then. Be home at Tawcester Towers in a couple of days.'

'No, we won't,' said Twinks coolly, carefully avoiding the reproach in her brother's eyes. 'Zammer Kabaret on Winkelstrasse. Nine of the jolly old clock. We will be there.'

'We?' Petrovsky echoed.

'Yes. Blotto and me.'

'Oh.' Count Kasimir Petrovsky looked as downcast as Blotto. The evening's assignation was going to be rather more crowded than the one he had had in mind.


Corky Froggett wasn't enjoying being in Berlin. He was finding it hard to break the mental habits engendered by four years in the trenches. For a finely tuned fighting machine like him to go out in public might represent a serious risk. He wasn't sure that he would be able to curb his instinct to shoot every German he encountered.

And Twinks had made it very clear to him that following that instinct would be *a very bad thing*.

So he stayed in his room in the cheap hotel behind the Adlon where the servants of the hotel's guests were stabled. He fumed with frustration. He was as keen as Blotto to get back to Tawcester Towers as soon as possible. He spent as long as he could in the Adlon's extensive underground garage, tuning the already perfectly tuned Lagonda. The rest of the time he just sat morosely in his room and waited for the summons from the young master.


The actions of the other chauffeur, Dmitri Raselov, were very different. On the Sunday morning he had passed a note to one of the Adlon's chefs and by midday he had had a reply. Following these instructions, he waited until after dark, then set off from his squalid hotel into the icy streets of Berlin.

He walked purposefully, certain of his destination. A few passers-by turned to marvel at his size, but he seemed unaware of them.

Some ten minutes away from the Adlon Raselov turned into a narrow shabby street. About half way along it he suddenly turned down some steps which led to a basement door over which a faded sign showed just the word 'Uli's'. He rapped out a coded knock and waited to be admitted.

Inside he found himself in a dimly lit bierkeller. Men, mostly wearing dark peasant smocks and some with Lenin caps, recognised the newcomer and raised their steins of beer to him.

'Good evening, Comrades,' said Dmitri Raselov.

## 12

# Excitements at the Zammer Kabaret

Corky Froggett's face showed no emotion when he was told he needed to drive his young master and mistress in the Lagonda to Winkelstrasse that evening. His hair and moustache bristled as usual. No one could have suspected the fury that he was repressing. They were not going straight back to Tawcester Towers and for him the torment of not being able to shoot any Germans was set to continue for some time.

Twinks had obtained directions to the Zammer Kabaret from the reception desk at the Adlon. She had noted that these had been given with a raised eyebrow, as if the receptionist did not think it was a suitable destination for well-bred foreign visitors. Corky had memorised the directions and he drove without hesitation through ever narrower and less salubrious streets towards Schöneberg and their meeting with Count Kasimir Petrovsky.

Blotto, in appropriate evening dress, noted with fore-boding the elaborate preparations that his sister had made for the evening. She was always glamorous, but when she pulled the stops out, she could look a real breathsapper. And she did that evening. She was not dressed in one of her short 'flapper' skirts, but in a full-length ball dress in silvery grey silk. The same colour was picked up in her long mink coat. She was also wearing the Lyminster

Diamonds, a necklace which was only aired on very special occasions.

All of this was a very bad sign so far as Blotto was concerned. He was used to men falling for his sister like pinged partridges, but on the rare occasions when she reciprocated their feelings it always spelt trouble. And the care she had lavished on her appearance that evening suggested she was more interested than was safe in Count Kasimir Petrovsky.

Corky Froggett parked in a narrow alley just off Nollendorfplatz. A discreetly lit sign above the doorway identified the Zammer Kabaret. As soon as the Lagonda came to a halt two burly men in long black leather coats stepped forward to it. Corky, fearing for the safety of his passengers, immediately reached forward to take his revolver out of the glove compartment. Hope glowed within him. If the Germans attacked the Lyminsters then he would be entirely justified in shooting them.

But, annoyingly, all the men in black did was to open the back door of the Lagonda to escort his charges into the club. At the door one led the new arrivals inside, while the other returned to the Lagonda and barked orders at him in German. Corky understood from the man's gestures that he was to park a little further along the street and, fuming with frustration, did as he was told.

He sat there in the car in a mood of suppressed fury, knowing he must leave his revolver in the glove compartment. His only hope was that, in a rough area like this, somebody might try to steal the Lagonda. If that happened, of course he would be fully within his rights to shoot the aspiring robber.

Inside the foyer of the Zammer Kabaret the doorman in black leather passed Blotto and Twinks over to a very glamorous woman with a rather firm jaw, prominent Adam's apple and a dress showing a lot of well-developed shoulder. White make-up was caked over her face, kohl surrounded her eyes and her plump lips were red. She led them to the reception desk, managed by another equally glamorous, strong-featured and heavily made-up woman. Here it was that entry tickets were sold, but when Twinks announced in fluent German that they were meeting Count Kasimir Petrovsky, their money was refused and they were led by yet another gloriously bedecked woman with an Adam's apple into the interior of the Kabaret.

The thick padded door which separated the foyer from the main room had muffled the noise but once they were inside Blotto and Twinks's ears were bombarded by the raucous brass of a jazz band. The musicians were at the back of a large stage which took over most of the central area. On three sides were small tables of diners and drinkers in immaculate evening dress. Rows of more tables behind spread back to the room's walls where private alcoves looked out towards the entertainment area.

Muscular waitresses in thick make-up, short black dresses, white aprons and fishnet stockings plied their way speedily between the tables, holding aloft trays of food and drink. Champagne appeared to be the tipple of choice for most of the customers.

Meanwhile on the central stage dancing girls danced. They were dressed in black, but very little of it. The thin strips of fabric across their tops and bottoms did nothing to hide their contours; in fact they drew attention to them. Blotto's eyes stood out on stalks. He was immobilised, so rooted to the spot that Twinks had to physically drag him towards the alcove from which Count Kasimir Petrovsky was beckoning to them.

Needless to say, he had a bottle of champagne in an ice bucket on the table. And needless to say, he had filled three glasses by the time they had reached him. He leant across to take Twinks's hand and plant on it a long and devoted kiss. He was wearing some kind of dress uniform, even more elaborate than the one he had had on that morning. Even more frogging. And no sword this time. Weapons were not allowed to be carried inside the Zammer Kabaret.

'It is so excellent to see you, Honoria,' he said. 'I have spent the day dreaming only of this moment.'

'It is good to see you too, Count. And please call me "Twinks".'

'"Twinks"? What is this?'

'It's just the tag that hangs round the young droplet's neck,' said Blotto. 'Everyone calls her "Twinks".'

'Very well. It is "Twinks" I will call you, in spite of believing that "Honoria" is a more beautiful name. Though of course,' he added with practised ease, 'neither name is as beautiful as the woman to whom it belongs.'

Blotto's sister smiled in a way which he wished looked rather less gratified than it did. If Twinks was falling in love with Count Kasimir Petrovsky, who could say when they'd ever leave Berlin?

Twinks took a seat next to the Count and looked around the room. The noise from the band was still overpoweringly loud. Smoke gathered in clouds towards the ceiling. The sparsely clad girls on stage were miming something that Blotto didn't recognise but which rather unsettled him. Twinks, from her researches in books rather than personal experience, knew exactly what they were miming. So did the Count, though his recognition came from vast experience.

'Why did you wish to meet here?' she asked him.

'The venue is unimportant. Anywhere where I meet you instantly becomes the most beautiful place in the world.'

'Oh, don't talk such toffee,' she said, but she had rather enjoyed his words. 'Why have you chosen this place if you want to speak of political secrets?'

'Political secrets are only part of the reason I am here. The main reason is for gazing once again on the perfection that is you.'

'What guff,' said Twinks. But she did still quite like it.

Before Count Kasimir Petrovsky could offer further compliments, Blotto intervened a little pettishly. 'Listen, my revered sis just asked you a perfectly four-square question. Why is this a good place to talk about political secrets? I think the decent thing would be to give her an answer.'

'Very well,' said the Count. 'There is an old Cossack proverb, which goes: "The safest place to hide is nearest to the searchlight." And in this case—'

'But that's a load of globbins,' Blotto objected. 'It doesn't fit the pigeon-hole at all. The nearer to the searchlight you are the more chance there is of someone clapping their peepers on you.'

'But what if you are in the shadow of the tower of the searchlight? Then you will not be seen.'

'Well, fair biddles. You may not be seen for a while, but at some point you're going to have to leave your hidey-hole and then the stenchers with the searchlight will mow you down like nettles in a nursery. I mean, if you—'

Count Kasimir Petrovsky was now getting a little pettish too. 'Look, we don't need to take the wretched proverb apart. I was just using it as an example of the fact that a public setting can often be a very good place for the exchange of secrets.' He gestured round the crowded Kabaret. 'Here the noise level is so high that nobody can hear anything anyone else is saying. More important, nobody is *interested* in what anyone else is saying. They are interested in guzzling food and drink or in who they're going to end up in bed with. For these two reasons it is the perfect place to pass on confidential information. But there is a third reason why I suggested we should meet here at the Zammer Kabaret. And that is because everyone in this room is a supporter of the White Russian cause!'

'Ah, good ticket,' said Blotto. 'On the same page with you now.'

'So now,' said Twinks, 'you give us the beans you couldn't spill at the Adlon coffee house this morning?'

'Precisely,' said the Count. 'But first we need more champagne!'

He snapped his fingers and immediately a tall glamorous waitress was at their table. Her black skirt seemed unfeasibly short and her fishnetted legs went on to the furthest point of the universe. Like the other women they had encountered in the Zammer Kabaret, she had heavy make-up and a very marked jawline.

She looked Blotto up and down and said something rather seductive in German. He looked for help to his sister. Twinks translated, 'She is saying what a handsome blond man you are and which part of Germany do you come from?'

The waitress quickly picked up the nationality she was dealing with and said to Blotto in a heavily accented voice, 'You are very good looking, big boy.'

He reddened. 'Oh, don't talk such sherry trifle.'

'It's true. I am called Jutta. Maybe at the end of the evening you like to come back to my place . . . ?'

'Why?' asked Blotto. 'What would I find at your place?'

'You would find me at my place.'

'Yes.' Blotto was confused. 'But I've just found you here. So why for the love of strawberries would I want to find you at your place?'

'You would find more of me at my place,' said Jutta in her sultriest tone.

'There seems to be plenty of you already. I'm not sure that—'

Count Kasimir Petrovsky had had enough of this banter. 'Get the champagne, girl!' he barked in German.

With a sulky pout, followed by a kiss blown to Blotto, Jutta, swinging her hips extravagantly, made her way through the crowds towards the bar.

'So, Count—'

'Please, call me Kasimir.'

'Very well, Kasimir. And you must promise you will always call me Twinks.'

'Very well, Twinks.'

'So you say everyone here tonight has White Russian sympathies?'

'Nearly everyone. Even here there will be a few Bolshevik spies. They are everywhere. But we have ways of dealing with them.'

'Oh, what ways?' asked Blotto.

'You do not wish to know what ways. But we are safe here. We can talk properly.'

'Good ticket,' said Twinks. 'So tell us about the White Russians and why you are here.'

'Very well.' The Count swept back his moustaches with both hands as he began his narrative. 'You know the history of the Russian Revolution and the subsequent Russian Civil War?'

'No,' said Blotto.

'Of course,' said Twinks.

'Well, this war was between the Red Army, led by the Bolsheviks and the Whites, an association of many organisations who had one thing in common – they were the enemies of the Bolsheviks and they wanted to restore some kind of Tsarist regime. This is my wish,' he said fervently. 'This is still the cause to which I will dedicate my life. It is for me the most important thing in the world!' He looked at Twinks. 'Or it was until today when I met the love of my life and suddenly a new imperative of extraordinary beauty is—'

'Yes, let's take that as read, shall we?' said Twinks. It wasn't that she was not enjoying his compliments, but she did really want to get on with things. 'The chock in the cogwheel is that you, the Whites, lost the Civil War, didn't you?'

'This is a source of great unhappiness to all of us, but it is undeniably true.'

'So the cause of the Whites,' said Blotto, wanting to contribute something to the conversation, 'is stuck up the Sewer of No Return.'

'So it might seem.' But Petrovsky's narrative was interrupted by the return of Jutta with a fresh bottle of champagne. While she opened it, she directed more lascivious looks towards Blotto, who giggled nervously.

Once she had wiggled away the Count continued, 'Yes, you may think that the cause of the Whites is destroyed forever, but this is not the case. We are not finished. There are many of us, scattered it is true throughout Europe and even some in America, but we are all passionate to return in triumph to our homeland. We hear tales of misery of how our people are faring under the cruel yoke of the Bolsheviks and it is our firm intention to restore the rightful regime to our Mother Russia!'

'Isn't there a bit of a problemette there?' Twinks suggested very tactfully.

'What problemette, my beloved?'

'Am I right that what you're gabbing on about is the restoration of the Romanov dynasty?'

'Of course.'

'Well, I thought . . .' she chose her words very delicately '. . . that events at Yekaterinburg might make that rather difficult.'

'Why is that?' asked Petrovsky.

'Well, not to fiddle around the furniture, there are no members of the Romanov dynasty with any puff left in them.'

'Ah. That is what is generally believed, yes.'

'Are you suggesting that someone managed to escape from that cellar in Yekaterinburg?'

'No, my angel. I am suggesting that somebody was not in the cellar in Yekaterinburg.'

'What do you mean? The Tsar and Tsarina had another child that nobody knew about?'

'No. The Tsarina was not involved.'

'Rein in the roans a moment,' said Blotto. 'I don't know a lot about this having babies rombooley, but I do know that having both parents involved at some point is the minimum requirement.'

'Is it not possible that one of the parents was not the Tsarina?' demanded Petrovsky.

'What, you mean that Tsar had been cornswiggling with another woman?' asked Twinks. 'But that would make the resultant offspring illegitimate.'

'It would if the Tsar was not married to the woman, yes.'

Twinks looked at the Count in amazement. 'Are you saying that the Tsarevich was already married before he married Her Grand Ducal Highness Princess Alix Victoria Helena Luise Beatrice of Hessa and by Rhine?' It was characteristic of Twinks that she should have such details at her fingertips.

Count Kasimir Petrovsky smiled knowingly.

'But surely he didn't marry his mistress, the St Petersburg ballerina Mathilde Kschessinska?'

'No, no, that was just an affair.'

'Then who for the love of strawberries did he twiddle up the old reef knot with?'

'You know that when he was young the Tsarevich would frequently visit his grandparents, King Christian IX and Queen Louise of Denmark.'

'Yes,' said Twinks, 'At Fredensborg Palace.'

'Precisely. Well, it was on one such visit, when he was about eighteen, that the Tsarevich became enamoured of one of his grandmother's ladies-in-waiting.'

'Toad-in-the-hole!' said Blotto.

'Her name was Countess Kirsten Jensen-Ibsen of Karlsen. For both of them it was like a flash of lightning. They fell for each other on sight – exactly as you and I did at the Hotel Adlon this morning, Twinks.'

She might have argued over quite how mutual the feelings had been that morning, but Twinks didn't want to interrupt Petrovsky's narrative, so she let it pass.

'With the Russian royal party at Fredensborg there was an Orthodox priest called Father Kyril Yakhunin, who was very close to the Tsarevich. He agreed to marry him secretly to the Countess. King Christian and Queen Louise got wind of what was going on and tried to stop the marriage. Father Yakhunin told them that their intervention had come in time, that nothing had happened. But he lied. By then the Tsarevich and the Countess were already married.

'Their families of course would not allow them to have any more to do with each other, but they had been together long enough for Kirsten to become pregnant. So she gave birth in secret to the Heir to the Tsar.'

'Toad-in-the-hole!' said Blotto.

'Are you telling me,' asked Twinks, 'that Nicholas's later marriage, to Her Grand Ducal Highness Princess Alix Victoria Helena Luise Beatrice of Hessa and by Rhine, was bigamous? That it had no legal validity?'

'That is exactly what I am telling you.'

'So is this boddo still around?' asked Blotto. 'You know, the son of Nicholas and the Countess?'

'He most certainly is. He is here in Berlin. He has spent his life under the name of Prince Evgeni Labatrov, but he should rightly be known as Tsar Evgeni I! Already he has a lot of support from White Russians here in Berlin. Also in Paris. And in other countries where White Russians gather – Finland, Estonia, Latvia, Lithuania – armies are mobilising to restore the Tsar's heir to his proper place. The powder keg is primed, the fuse is just waiting to be lit. Then the evil Bolshevik regime will be overturned. Russian aristocrats will reclaim the estates which were stolen from them. And Prince Evgeni Labatrov will be crowned as Tsar Evgeni I!

'And,' Count Kasimir Petrovsky concluded triumphantly, 'he will lead the White Russians to victory against the vile hordes of the Bolsheviks!'

## 13

# Unwelcome Guests

While these dramatic events were unfolding inside the Zammer Kabaret, outside Corky Froggett waited miserably in the Lagonda, still feeling the pain of being prevented from doing what he had been so carefully trained to do. To add to his troubles, it was by then extremely cold and, though he would never had admitted to such weakness, he wished he had a coat to put on over his thin chauffeur's uniform.

Not far away from Corky, his fellow driver Dmitri Raselov was still in the bierkeller. He had been drinking since he arrived – vodka not beer in his case – but the alcohol appeared to have no effect on him.

He felt cheerful and secure. For, just as the Zammer Kabaret was a safe house for White Russians, so Uli's Bierkeller was a refuge for the Reds. Though Dmitri had not previously met all of the other customers he knew that everyone present shared the same ambitions. They wanted to further the cause of communism by liquidating everyone with any connection to the Romanov regime. It was comforting for him to be among like-minded people.

Finally the man Dmitri Raselov had been waiting for arrived in Uli's Bierkeller. Small in stature, he wore the regulation dark peasant smock and Lenin cap. His beard and moustache were also modelled on those of the deceased Bolshevik leader. When Raselov was pointed out to him, the man came straight across with hand outstretched. 'Good evening, Comrade,' he said. 'I am Fyodor Vlachko.'

When, at about three o'clock in the morning, Twinks announced that she and Blotto should return to the Adlon, Count Kasimir Petrovsky was desolated. 'I cannot be parted from you so soon after we have met! The flame of my love cannot so soon be exposed to buffeting by the winds of loneliness! My soul will shrivel and die like a plant in the desert without water!'

'Oh, don't talk such toffee,' said Twinks. 'We can meet up again tomorrow.'

'Actually, Twinks me old candle-snuffer,' said Blotto, 'I'm not sure that we can. Corky Froggett and I were thinking that an early start back to Tawcester Towers might fit the pigeon-hole.'

'No,' said his sister in a voice which made her sound very much like her mother. And had exactly the same effect on Blotto as a prohibition from the Dowager Duchess would have done.

He didn't argue. He just muttered, 'Oh, rodents!'

And turned his eyes to the performance onstage. There two real German Shepherd dogs and two men dressed as German Shepherd dogs were doing things to German *fräuleins* dressed in very little. Blotto, whose knowledge encompassed the training of hounds for hunting, wondered how on earth the German shepherds had been trained to do what they were doing on that stage.

'Right,' said Twinks. 'Time we pongled off.'

When they were seen to be rising from the table, the waitress Jutta swept across to them. Ignoring Twinks and Petrovsky, she turned the full beam of her attention on Blotto.

'So you are leaving, big boy? If you wait half an hour, I will have finished my shift. You can join me then.'

'That is an excellent idea,' said Petrovsky, envisaging an opportunity of being alone with Twinks.

'I think probably the right ticket for me is a bit of the old shut-eye,' said Blotto.

Jutta thrust out her lower lip in an elaborate pout. 'But it is early,' she protested. 'Here in Berlin the evening is only just starting. You come back with me and I can show you things that you never have expected to see in your life.'

'That is certainly true,' the Count murmured to Twinks, who let out a little giggle.

'Oh, come on, big boy,' Jutta persisted. 'I can take you somewhere where your every wish will be fulfilled.'

'Really?' said Blotto, beginning to sound rather enthused.

'Of course I can.'

'Hoopee-doopee!' said Blotto. 'I didn't know anyone played cricket out here.'

Jutta looked at him blankly as Twinks took his arm and said, 'Time we were moving, Blotto me old egg-coddler.'

'We meet again, big boy?' asked Jutta, apparently desolated.

'Who knows?' replied Blotto. 'Hounds often return to the same vomit, don't they?'

Jutta looked totally confused.

As they were getting their coats, Blotto chuckled. 'That waitress was a bit of a rum baba, wasn't she? I don't think I've ever clapped my peepers on a woman like that before.'

'No,' Twinks agreed. 'I don't think you have.'


Compared to the bulk of Dmitri Raselov, Fyodor Vlachko was a small man, but there was no doubt who was the dominant personality in the relationship. Vlachko was an officer of the Cheka and spymaster of the Reds in Berlin, said to be constantly in direct communication with the Kremlin.

Raselov listened spellbound as his boss listed the tasks to be achieved. The giant was excited. Finally all the tedium and frustration of the last two years, all of the cosying up to pernicious, culturally contemptible White Russians like Count Konstantin Krupkov, would be at an end. He would never have to return to the politically unacceptable world of London. Vlachko assured Raselov that his efforts had been appreciated, that they had been commended and would not be forgotten by the highest authorities in the Kremlin.

But now was the time for him to embark on the mission for which all this undercover work had been preparation. The huge man leant forward, listening intently as Vlachko gave him his instructions.


'I actually,' said Blotto, 'am a bit of a lip-licker for big girls.'

'I know,' said Twinks as a silent, still frustrated Corky Froggett drove them through the dark, icy streets of Berlin.

'Always like the kind of filly who could come off a hunter over a high hedge and still bounce up like a good 'un.'

'Yes.'

He said nothing for a moment. Then, very casually, he announced, 'Might think of going back to the Zammer Kabaret at some point . . .'

'To see Jutta again?'

'Oh,' he said, elaborately surprised. 'The idea hadn't drifted into the old brainbox that she'd be there. But I suppose she might . . .'

Twinks contemplated saying something, but curbed the instinct. She was hatching a plan whereby Blotto and Corky should start the journey back to Tawcester Towers the following day – or in fact when she thought about it, later that day. She, on the other hand, might stay on in

Berlin to get to know Count Kasimir Petrovsky rather better. He had said he would leave a note at the Adlon reception about where they might meet for lunch.

Corky Froggett decanted them from the Lagonda in front of the Adlon's main entrance. Immediately uniformed doormen came to usher them inside. The air seemed to have got colder during their journey from the Zammer Kabaret. It stung their faces and the trees of Unter den Linden sparkled with frost.

In the welcome warmth of the foyer, as they collected their keys one of the men behind the reception counter said that a letter had been delivered for them and handed it across to Twinks. She tore open the envelope in the lift as the liftman clanked the double doors across and set the machine in motion to take them up to the third floor.

The letter was written in Russian, which of course she understood perfectly.

It read: 'Come and collect these sponging Bashuskys. I want them out of my house as soon as possible! Pavel Lewinsky.'

14

# Plots and Counterplots

Twinks was up bright and early a few hours later. Having breakfasted in her suite and dressed in a rather chic tweed suit, she had first checked on the telephone to reception as to whether a note had been left for her by Petrovsky. Nothing had arrived, but then she reassured herself that they'd only parted a few hours before.

Then she went across the landing to bang on the door of Blotto's suite. He was in a less sparkling mood. Her knocking had woken him from a very complicated and rather unsettling dream which had involved two German Shepherds, Mephistopheles and Jutta wearing only two thin bands of black ribbon. As consciousness returned he was aware that the interior of his head felt like a stable that hadn't been mucked out for a fortnight.

'Come on, Blotters me old tin of tooth powder,' said Twinks, offensively cheery for that hour of the morning. 'I've sent a message for Corky to have the Lagonda round the front in ten mins. So gird up the old loins and encase the doughty limbs in the armour of tweed. We have to find out what new glue pot the Bashuskys have dunked themselves into. Now, do you want me to order you some breakfast?'

The green look on Blotto's face prompted by that suggestion told her that the answer was a no.

* * *

Blotto didn't look much more robust when the Lagonda drew up on the gravel drive of the Lewinsky mansion. Because his head was in his hands he couldn't take in the splendour and scale of the house, but Twinks was suitably impressed. It looked more like a palace than a private residence, with space to accommodate any number of poor relations. Clearly the Lewinskys had managed to get a great deal of money out of Russia before the Bolsheviks took over.

She hardly had time for this thought, however, because she saw on the front steps of the mansion, looking very bedraggled and sorry for themselves, the four Bashuskys. With their luggage. They'd been turned out of the house like kleptomaniac servants.

Corky Froggett vacated the driving seat and started to put their shabby valises into the Lagonda's dickie. A still-bleary Blotto and a still-sparkling Twinks also left the car to sort out how they were going to get four more people into it.

Count Igor Bashusky, as ever, looked aggrieved. Once again the world had not treated him with the deference that he believed to be his due. 'These people are charlatans.' he said. 'You tell us they are members of the Romanov family. They are that no more than we are. Their name is Lewinsky. They are just ... *bankers*.' The level of contempt he managed to infuse into that single word was enormous. The fact that the Bashuskys themselves had no money did not prevent them from despising people who actually worked with the stuff.

'Did something happen?' asked Twinks. 'Did something particularly inky blot your copybook for them to throw you out so unceremoniously?'

'Not at all,' the Count replied. 'We behaved as befits a family of Russian aristocrats.'

'That is untrue!' The new voice came from a short man in a velvet smoking jacket who had just burst out of the mansion's front door. Twinks somehow knew he had to be

Pavel Lewinsky. He spoke in Russian, in which of course she was as proficient as she was in German (and Japanese and Mandarin, come to that).

'These people are confidence tricksters!' he went on. 'They come, take my hospitality, eat my food, drink my vodka – in very large measures – and I tolerate this because I have been told they are members of the Romanov family!'

'We were told you were members of the Romanov family!' Count Igor protested. Twinks was by now fully aware of how much chaos the small lies of Professor Erasmus Holofernes had caused.

'They are not Romanovs. They are spongers of the first order.' Pavel Lewinsky went on, 'They have treated not only my servants, but also members of my own family with appalling arrogance. And all the time they stand in front of the fireplace so nobody else can get any heat from the fire!'

Yes, thought Twinks wryly, that's the Bashuskys for you.

'But their worst crime,' Pavel Lewinsky continued, his fury increasing with every word, 'was committed by that apology for a human being!' His finger pointed unerringly to Sergei Bashusky. The young man looked pimplier than ever.

'He had the audacity to break unbidden into the boudoir of my only daughter and to threaten her honour!'

'That is not true,' Sergei protested. 'Natasha invited me to join her in her boudoir. And,' he couldn't resist adding, 'into her bedroom.'

'Silence!' roared Pavel Lewinsky. 'I do not wish to hear the name of my daughter on the lips of such a degenerate!'

'But I love Natasha!' cried Sergei Bashusky. This was the best news Twinks had heard all morning. If he had fallen for someone else, then he would no longer be addressing his threats of suicide to her.

As if to prove the point, Sergei cried, 'If I cannot be with Natasha, I will kill myself!'

'Very good news!' said Pavel Lewinsky. 'Then there will only be three of you sponging Bashuskys left in the world!'

'I mean what I say, and I—'

But Sergei's protestation was cut off in mid-flow by the eruption from the front door of a very pretty dark-haired girl in her late teens, crying, 'Papa, you cannot ever separate me from Sergei!'

Twinks, who was quite acute about that kind of thing, deduced that the new arrival must be Natasha Lewinsky.

And so it proved when the girl rushed across to throw her arms around the lanky, knobbly figure of Sergei Bashusky. 'We love each other!' she shouted over her shoulder to her father. 'We can never be separated! Our love is as powerful as a mighty river, sweeping away everything else in its path!'

For a moment Twinks had a thought that the girl might, like Count Kasimir Petrovsky, have learned her English from romantic novels, then quickly reminded herself that Natasha was actually speaking in Russian. And she got the feeling that perhaps the Russians spoke like that all the time.

Pavel Lewinsky opened the front door and called out, 'Roman! Arkadi!'

Two heavy-set uniformed flunkeys appeared.

Lewinsky pointed towards his daughter and gave the order, 'Take her inside! Lock her in her room!'

Though Natasha clung to Sergei like a limpet, the two servants peeled her off him and took her, wailing and protesting, back into the house. Her young lover looked sorrowfully after her. Bearing in mind the previous response it had had from Natasha's father, he didn't repeat his suicide threat.

Pavel Lewinsky looked at his watch. 'I will come out again in five minutes and I will be carrying a gun. If any of you . . .' he pointed to the Bashuskys '. . . or you . . .' he pointed to Blotto, Twinks and Corky '. . . are still here, I will shoot you.' And he went back inside his house.

Corky turned eagerly to the young master and the young mistress. 'He's threatened to kill you. And I know he's a Russian rather than a German, but surely that gives me an excuse to shoot him?'

'Well, I'm not sure,' said Blotto. 'It's a ticklish point of etiquette in—'

'No,' said Twinks. Once again it was in her mother's voice. Corky Froggett didn't argue.

When they were all squashed inside the Lagonda, Twinks asked the Bashuskys if they'd thought what their next step might be.

'Well, it is obvious,' Count Igor replied. 'We will stay at the Adlon until you take us back to Tawcester Towers.'

The Blotto and Twinks who returned to the hotel were grim-faced. Both were thinking the same. How could they ever face the Dowager Duchess if they returned home and the Bashuskys were still with them? This time they were up to their necks in the treacle.

# 15

# The Heir to the Tsar

There was no way round it. Rooms had to be booked in the Adlon for the Bashuskys. The Lyminster account would be drained even further as their unwanted guests played fast and loose with the Room Service menu.

The only good thing that happened, from Twinks's point of view, was that she managed a quick word with Sergei in the hotel foyer. 'You are in love with Natasha Lewinsky?' she asked.

'Yes, I will love her till I die.'

'And that won't be too soon, I hope?'

'What do you mean?'

'When you claimed to be in love with me – only yesterday – you kept talking a lot about committing suicide.'

'Yes, but that was because you denied me your love. You did not love me too. Natasha loves me. We are destined to be together forever.'

'Oh, larksissimo,' said Twinks. 'Congratulations!'

He looked into her eyes, but no light was kindled in his own. 'You would never have been suitable for me,' he announced. 'You are far too old.' And he set off towards the lift to find his new room.

Twinks did not bother to be insulted by his words. Relief that she would no longer have Sergei drooping around making cow's eyes at her all the time was a much stronger emotion.

She was also cheered by the fact that there now was a message at reception for her from Count Kasimir Petrovsky. He said he would send a car at twelve thirty to take her from the Adlon to his favourite restaurant, *Die Jagdhütte*. 'And I mean *you*. It is your company I wish to enjoy for luncheon, so lose the idiot brother!'

That was not going to be difficult. The interior of Blotto's head now felt like a stable that hadn't been mucked out for a month. He was only fit for ordering a bottle of brandy to be delivered to his suite and, after a few therapeutic hairs of the dog, returning to his bed.

Twinks felt a *frisson* of excitement at the thought of lunching with Petrovsky on his own.

She then looked at the last paragraph of his note. 'And after we have enjoyed our afternoon,' it read, 'I wish to introduce you – and your brother this time – to the Heir to the Tsar. Prince Evgeni Labatrov will be in Mitzi's Bar on Klutzdamstrasse at seven o'clock this evening.'

Twinks passed on this information to Blotto before he staggered back up to his suite. 'Remember the name, Blotters. Prince Evgeni Labatrov. In Mitzi's Bar on Klutzdamstrasse. Seven o'clock this evening.'

'Bleargh,' said Blotto.

Then Twinks looked at the last words of the note. 'I am counting the minutes till I am once more in your glorious presence, my angel. All my love, Kasimir.'

She felt a warm glow of anticipation, and went up to her suite to slip into something breathsappingly stunning.

At the cheap hotel behind the Adlon, Corky Froggett sat on his bed in a state of undiminished frustration. The night before, the young master had mumbled something about possibly returning to Tawcester Towers that day. But as yet no summons had come. And Corky still didn't trust himself to go out on to the streets of Berlin. Too many Germans around.

At some point during the late morning there was a tap on the door of his room. He leapt up to open it, anticipating the go-ahead message from Blotto, and was disappointed to find Dmitri Raselov looming in the doorway.

'Please, I wonder,' asked the Russian in his halting English, 'do you know where are Bashusky family? They stay, I think, with relations here in Berlin . . . ?'

'Not any more they don't,' said Corky. 'Rather blotted their copybooks there, I'm afraid. Got turned out. They are once again staying in the Hotel Adlon.'

'Thank you. That is very good.' And as Raselov turned to return to his own room, an evil smile played around his lips. They really were making the job easy for him.

Of course Twinks knew that *Die Jagdhütte* meant 'The Hunting Lodge' and the interior of the restaurant in the centre of Berlin was decorated to make the customers feel they were in the middle of a forest. The entire space was wood-panelled, the heads of flamboyantly antlered stags were mounted on the walls, and log fires crackled.

It was clear that Count Kasimir Petrovsky was a familiar and well-liked regular. Waiters bowed and scraped to him in a manner that was just the right side of obsequious. He knew the menu and the wine list well enough to order without looking at them.

And he was, Twinks thought once again, an extraordinarily good-looking man. Armed with another glass of champagne, she settled back to enjoy whatever the afternoon might bring.

Blotto woke about five, feeling immeasurably better and as hungry as Mephistopheles at the end of a day's hunting.

He thought of going down to one of the Hotel Adlon's restaurants to stoke himself up but, aware of the danger of meeting a Bashusky, ordered from Room Service instead. A large venison steak and a bottle of a rather good Côtes du Rhône quickly brought him back to zing-zing condition.

And by then it was time to slip into the evening penguin garb and pongle down to Mitzi's Bar on Klutzdamstrasse. Wherever that might be. Seven o'clock, Twinks had said.

He asked at reception where he'd find Mitzi's Bar on Klutzdamstrasse and when told it was only a few streets away decided to continue the head-clearing process by walking there. No need to make Corky Froggett get the Lagonda out for a little job like that. Feeling rather magnanimous for not bothering the chauffeur, he set off into the cold night, not realising that he had in fact condemned Corky to an evening of even greater frustration.

Though without any big display outside, Mitzi's Bar on Klutzdamstrasse proved easy to find. Two large doormen stood at the door. Bulges under their overcoats suggested that they were well-armed. And they seemed extremely unwilling to let Blotto in.

They had enough English to keep asking him rather difficult questions like why he had come to the bar. He didn't really know the answer. His hangover that morning had been so ferocious he hadn't taken in everything that Twinks had said to him in the Adlon foyer. He'd remembered the address all right, but the rest of her words had been erased by the fuzziness of alcohol.

Then it came back to him that he was meant to be meeting someone. And the boddo's name was Prince Evgeni Somethingorother. Still the doormen seemed suspicious. It was only when he mentioned he was also meant to be meeting Count Kasimir Petrovsky that they let him pass.

Once inside, giving his cloak to the hatcheck girl who spoke in her native tongue, he suddenly realised he was alone with no German-speaking sister to support him. Undaunted, he resorted to the familiar English backstop position of talking very slowly and loudly. He felt rather pleased with himself because the girl clearly understood that he wanted her to take his cloak.

He used a similar technique at the bar, adding pointing at the relevant bottle to his repertoire of talking very slowly and loudly. He looked around the smoky interior but saw no sign of Twinks or Petrovsky. So, having braced himself with a couple of large brandies, Blotto asked the barman – very slowly and loudly – whether a pineapple called Prince Evgeni Somethingorother had been in that evening.

If the barman had any English, he wasn't going to waste it on Blotto. With a jerk of his elbow he indicated a table in the darkest corner of the bar.

Before he approached them, Blotto took stock of the people sitting there. A man with a voluminous grey beard which almost hid the cross hanging round his neck wore a long black robe and a cylindrical black hat. Of the rest some wore army uniforms and some evening dress. There was a thin man in a plain black day suit, whose pale blue eyes peered through tiny metal-rimmed glasses. But the focus of the group seemed to be a young man whose military-style costume and carefully trimmed beard emphasised any physical likeness he might have had to the deceased Nicholas II.

That, Blotto concluded, must be Prince Evgeni Labatrov, the Heir to the Tsar. He also noted the slightly petulant set of the young man's mouth.

Having armed himself with another double brandy, Blotto ambled across to the table. 'Well, how're you tootling, me old Comrades?' he greeted them.

His words sparked instant movement. The two burly men either side of the Prince immediately drew pistols and stood protectively in front of him. There was a clash of metal as others got up and drew their sabres. Blotto felt his arms grasped fiercely and the point of a dagger pressed against his Adam's apple.

117

'So why are you here, you filthy Red spy?' a voice hissed in his ear. But since it was talking in Russian, he hadn't a clue what it was on about.

'Look, I've no wish to harm any of you boddoes,' Blotto protested. 'Violence is just not my length of banana.'

The thin man with glasses said in a soft, insinuating voice (and in English), 'You are English?'

'Yes. Can't you tell?'

'Why should I be able to tell?'

'Well, I mean . . .' The thin man seemed to Blotto to be rather slow on the uptake '. . . look at me.'

'Your colouring is not particularly English. You could be Scandinavian, German, Russian even.'

'Oh come on, surely just one spoffing look at me ought to tell you that I'm not foreign.'

'Anyway, this is not important,' said the thin man. 'What matters is why you come here to attack us.'

'I didn't come here to attack you.'

'No? You are clearly in sympathy with the Reds. Why else did you call us "Comrades"?'

'Oh, is that what's started all this rombooley?'

'Here in Germany the only people who use the word "Comrade" are communists, Bolsheviks, scum of that kind.'

'Well, I can assure you,' said Blotto, 'that I've never had anything to do with lowlife like that.'

'What then are your politics?'

It was not a question that had ever been put to Blotto before, nor indeed one that he'd ever contemplated an answer to. 'Well,' he replied eventually, 'I'm aristocratic.'

'And what does that mean in terms of policy?'

'It means I believe that as aristocrats we are naturally born to rule and that oikish spongeworms like factory workers or Socialists should never be allowed to get near to the seat of political power.'

These were the first words he'd said that the thin man thought worthy of translation into Russian. When they understood Blotto's answer, the atmosphere relaxed considerably. There were cheers around the table, pistols were reholstered, sabres resheathed and Blotto's arms released.

'Good,' said the thin man. 'You are our kind of person. Please sit down. Pour vodka for our guest!'

Blotto sat down and swallowed the remains of his brandy before turning to the vodka which had been thrust on him.

'We still do not know your name,' said the thin man.

'I am the Lord Devereux Lyminster, but everyone calls me "Blotto".'

'Very well. It is a pleasure to meet you, Blotto.'

'Mutual biddles,' said Blotto. 'Sorry, didn't hear your name-tag.'

'I am Yuri Guriakin. And let me introduce the others around the table.'

This he did. Amidst the flurry of Russian names, the only two Blotto retained were those of the priest Father Kyril Yakhunin and of Prince Evgeni Labatrov, whom he had correctly identified as the Heir to the Tsar. The priest, he remembered from what Petrovsky had said, had some connection with the Prince, though the detail of what it was had slipped Blotto's mind.

After the introduction, a toast was drunk in vodka. Straight down in one. The interior of Blotto's throat was lightly seared, like a very rare steak.

Then Yuri Guriakin said, 'But, Blotto, you still have not told us why you are here.'

'I was just told to come to Mitzi's Bar on Klutzdamstrasse where I'd meet Prince Evgeni Somethingorother.'

'Who told you this?'

'Twinks.'

'Who is Twinks?'

'My sister.'

Guriakin looked mystified. 'I don't believe I know your sister. Was there no one else involved in sending you here?'

'Oh yes, of course.'

119

'Who?'

'Count Kasimir Petrovsky.'

Everyone at the table recognised the name and the atmosphere relaxed even further. Another vodka toast was drunk, this time to Petrovsky. Then somebody said that it was ungentlemanly for them not to have another toast to Blotto's sister. So Twinks was duly toasted.

'I look forward to meeting her,' said Prince Evgeni Labatrov. This was the first time he had acknowledged Blotto's presence. He spoke very good English, with an accent that carried overtones of British public school.

Blotto commented on this. 'Yes,' said the Prince. 'For part of my education, I was at Harrow.'

'Oh, bad luck,' said Blotto. It was the instinctive response of an Old Etonian, for whom rivalry with Harrovians was as dominant a gene as red hair.

'But I got tired of the discipline,' said the Heir to the Tsar. 'And the schoolmasters did not pay proper respect to my high status. So I left.'

'And what do you do now?' asked Blotto. It was not a question he would have put to an English aristocrat. He knew that no respectable English aristocrat ever did anything. But he suspected rules might be slacker among the continentals. There titles were invented with the same lavish abandon as over-extravagant military uniforms. No foreign aristocrats were really the genuine article.

Prince Evgeni Labatrov was, nonetheless, offended by the enquiry. 'I do, of course, nothing,' he replied, 'as befits my station in life. I do nothing but wait.'

'Do you, by Denzil?' said Blotto. 'And what is it you're waiting for?'

'I am waiting to return in glory to St Petersburg, and as a Romanov to sit on the Imperial Throne which is mine by right!'

'Good ticket,' murmured Blotto. He looked round the table. 'And all of you boddoes are going to help make that happen?'

Seeming to have no problem understanding his English, the White Russians cheered their approval.

'We will get the outcome we require,' said Yuri Guriakin. 'It is only a matter of patience. We have lived through a long time of inaction, but the moment for action is now not far away. All around the world White Russians yearn to return to Mother Russia. The Bolshevik swine have reduced our country to famine and poverty. The people cry out for help, for stability. We will provide that. White Russians around the world will soon be mobilising for the final push that will restore the Romanovs to the imperial throne in the form of Tsar Evgeni I!'

This bit of tub-thumping again prompted enthusiastic cheers. Blotto, in his usual slow way, came to the conclusion that Mitzi's Bar on Klutzdamstrasse must be a White Russian stronghold. Nobody seemed to be making any secret of their political affiliations.

'But for us, Blotto,' said Yuri Guriakin confidentially, 'the most important task we face is to ensure the security of the Heir to the Tsar. He is the icon around whom the forces of the White Russians will gather. We guard him like a precious jewel. Everyone around this table would give up their life to protect him. That was why we were so suspicious of you when you arrived and called us "Comrades". We thought you were an assassin sent by the Reds.'

'Well, I'm spoffing well not!' said Blotto.

'No, we worked that out. But you are a supporter of our cause?'

'Tickey-tockey,' said Blotto. 'Give me Whites over Reds any day.'

'Good. And you will join us when our armies march into Mother Russia?'

'Ah. Might be a bit inconvenient,' said Blotto. 'Must be pongling back to the old family seat before too long.'

'Yes, but—'

Yuri Guriakin's words were cut off by the entrance of Count Kasimir Petrovsky, looking more debonair and pleased with himself than ever. He was greeted with loud enthusiasm by all around the table. He bowed elaborately to Prince Evgeni Labatrov. 'Good evening, Your Highness,' he said.

Then he saw Blotto. 'And good evening to you too.'

'Where's Twinks? Did she pootle back to the Adlon after lunch?'

The Count smiled. 'No, after lunch she . . .' He seemed to recollect himself and not continue with what he was saying. 'She is here. She is just adjusting her make-up, I believe. One does not like to ask too closely what ladies do when they retire to the powder room. She will be with us shortly.' He pressed a heartfelt hand across the sash on his front. 'And every moment out of her presence weighs like an hour upon me.'

'Tickey-tockey,' said Blotto. 'Good ticket.'

'Petrovsky,' said Prince Evgeni Labatrov, 'I did not much like the girl you set up for me to have dinner with yesterday.'

'But she was from one of the most distinguished Russian families, Your Highness. Her parents are—'

'I don't care about that. The important thing was that the girl wasn't very pretty.'

'She has a reputation as being one of the beauties of Berlin.'

'Well, I didn't find her very pretty,' said the Prince pettishly.

'I apologise, Your Highness. I will endeavour to do better next time.'

'You'd better. Put your mind to it, Petrovsky. I don't like being served up with the ugly ones like that.'

Blotto was appalled. The idea of discussing any woman in public offended his sense of honour. It was just not the sort of thing that boddoes of the decent sort ever did. Yet here was the prospective Tsar of all the Russias bandying about the name of a woman from his own class in a public bar. And Count Kasimir Petrovsky was making no adverse comment about such behaviour.

Blotto was beginning to think perhaps he should make some tart observation, but he was prevented by Petrovsky saying, 'I apologise, Your Highness. It will not happen again.'

The Prince nodded curtly and downed another glass of vodka. He seemed restless and bored. His mood unsettled the others at the table. They looked nervous, not sure who would be the next recipient of his ire.

Suddenly he said, 'And I do have your loyalty, don't I? All of you. Your allegiance?'

They almost fell over each other in their assertions of their loyalty and allegiance.

'Because I am watching all of you. If I suspect anyone of betraying me, I will not hesitate to have them shot.'

This was greeted by a round of applause. 'He's a real Romanov,' said Father Kyril Yakhunin fondly.

'You are all here to protect me,' the Prince went on. 'That is your only role in life.'

'And it is a role we are honoured to undertake,' said Petrovsky smoothly. Blotto was rather disappointed to see the Count toadying to this spoilt brat.

'You would lay down your life for me?' asked the Prince, who seemed to require constant reassurance.

'That too would be an honour,' said Petrovsky. 'The greatest honour that can be bestowed upon a servant of the Tsar.'

At that moment Twinks entered the room. She had dressed with extraordinary care for her lunch at *Die Jagdhütte* and whatever she had done to her make-up in the powder room had only added to her allure. Blotto didn't know how his sister had spent the afternoon, but whatever she'd been doing had prevented her from changing into evening wear. But it also seemed to have given her an extra sparkle. Even from the perspective of a brother, he had to admit that, the way she looked that evening, she was a bit of a breathsapper.

She seemed to have an even stronger effect on the assembled White Russians. Not least on Prince Evgeni Labatrov. 'Well, now this is something!' he said. 'Who is the young lady?'

Petrovsky was about to answer, but Twinks intervened clearly in her cut-crystal voice. 'I can answer for myself, thank you. I am the Lady Honoria Lyminster, sister of the Duke of Tawcester.'

'Proper breeding as well as looks.' The Prince smiled across at Petrovsky. 'You have done well this time.'

'What do you mean, Your Highness?'

'I mean that this woman is beautiful enough even for my tastes. Have her delivered to my room at . . .' he checked his watch '. . . eleven o'clock precisely.'

'No, Your Highness.'

'What? Are you disobeying me, Petrovsky?'

'Yes, I am, Your Highness. This is not a woman to be handled like a chattel or commodity.'

'How right you are, Kazzy,' said Twinks. 'I am a free Englishwoman and what I do in life is what I spoffing well choose to do!'

Prince Evgeni Labatrov looked darkly at the Count. 'This is not a woman you have found for me, Petrovsky?'

'No, it is certainly not! If Twinks belongs to anyone—'

'Which I most certainly don't!' she asserted.

'It is to me!' Petrovsky continued.

'But I want her,' said the Prince, 'and I am the Heir to the Tsar!'

'Well, bad luck,' said Twinks, 'because I am not available.'

'No,' Petrovsky echoed. 'She is not available.'

'No, by the Great Wilberforce,' said Blotto, feeling he ought to get in on the act. 'My sister is not available.'

The Prince's face had turned to pure evil as he said, 'Are you confronting me, Petrovsky? Are you arguing with the will of the Tsar of all the Russias?'

'Yes!' said the Count. 'That is exactly what I am doing.'

'That is a very unwise course of action.' The Prince's voice was now icy cold and deadly. 'No one defies me and gets away with it.' He appealed to the men sitting around him. 'I still have your support, do I not, against this rebel?'

They didn't all sound completely convinced but the consensus was with the Prince.

'So, Petrovsky,' he said, 'what do you plan to do now?'

'I plan to do this!' The Count pulled a glove from his belt and slapped it hard across the face of the Heir to the Tsar. 'I challenge you to a duel for Twinks!'

'And I accept your challenge!'

The Prince turned for a muttered consultation with Yuri Guriakin, then faced his challenger again. 'Six o'clock tomorrow morning. Pistols. In the Tiergarten by the statue of Johann Wolfgang von Goethe. Yuri will be my second.'

'And mine will be . . .' Petrovsky looked around in some desperation before saying, 'the Lord Devereux Lyminster.'

'Oh, Hoopee-doopee!' said Blotto.


This contretemps had put a damper on the proceedings and after it the guests at the table rather melted away. As Blotto and Twinks were collecting their coats, Twinks heard Father Kyril Yakhunin speaking to one of the other men.

'Did you hear what he said, Blotters?'

'Well, I heard it, but he was gabbing in Russia, wasn't he? I haven't got a mouse squeak of an idea what he was pootling on about.'

'He said, "Pity about Petrovsky. He was a good man. But he is far too loyal to harm a hair of the head of the Heir to the Tsar. So he will aim with his pistol to miss the Prince. Tomorrow morning he will die!"'

16

# A Deadly Duel

It was very icy in the Tiergarten the next morning. The trees, outlined in frost, rose ghostly out of the low-lying white mist. Daylight had not yet fully asserted itself over the night. Blotto wished he were still tucked up in his huge soft bed at the Adlon.

But he wasn't. He was doing his duty supporting his new friend, Count Kasimir Petrovsky. And although he had been told that duelling was now illegal in Germany, this was an affair of honour and trying to back out of it would be the action of the worst kind of milk-livered stencher. Certainly not the action of the Lord Devereux Lyminster.

So he gritted his teeth and put up with the cold. Petrovsky had brought a bottle of brandy with him and frequent swigging from that helped.

Twinks was not with them. Although she was furious at being excluded, there was a consensus that duelling was man's work and the presence of any woman – even one as intrepid and resourceful as Twinks – was rather beyond the barbed wire. She would still have quite happily defied convention and joined the party in the Tiergarten, had Petrovsky himself not made her swear that she'd stay in the Adlon until the proceedings were completed.

Blotto took his responsibilities seriously and did his best in the role of second. He reckoned it was his job to jolly his man along, give him the illusion that he had a snowball's chance in hell of still being alive when seven o'clock struck. Though, what he had heard from Father Kyril Yakhunin the previous night did not make that seem a very likely outcome.

Still, Blotto went through the motions. 'Chinny-up, Petrovsky me old shoehorn,' he said. 'This is probably one of those duels which stop when the first blood is drawn.'

'No, it is not,' said the Count. 'It is to the death.'

'Oh, tough ticket,' said Blotto. 'Still, you never know which side up your toast's going to land, do you? You and the Prince might just go on missing each other.'

'This is unlikely. Prince Evgeni Labatrov has been trained as a pistol shooter by the best teachers in Europe. He can hit a moving target at five hundred metres. It is part of his education as the Heir to the Tsar.'

'But you yourself're probably a bit of a top-ranker when it comes to shooting.'

'I fear not. My weapon of choice – as befits a Cossack – is the sabre. If we were fighting with sabres, no one would have a chance against me.'

'Well . . .' Blotto looked into the murk beyond the statue of Goethe where a knot of dark-suited men stood around the Prince and Yuri Guriakin. 'Perhaps you could change the rules? Tick the box marked "sabre" rather than the one marked "pistol"?'

'No. The opposition dictated the terms – as it is their right to do. And I accepted them in front of witnesses.'

'Ah.' Blotto tried to find some small crumb of comfort in the situation. 'You never know your boodles,' he said. 'Perhaps, before he gets the opportunity to shoot you, the Prince will be carried off into the sky by some giant bird . . . ?'

'Yes,' said Petrovsky sarcastically. 'But in the unlikely event of that not happening, I must prepare to face my fate.' He grabbed Blotto by the lapels of his coat and pulled him very close. 'It is important you give this message to Twinks.'

'No probs, me old carpet-beater.'

'You must tell her that I love her more than anyone has ever loved before, that we have known a height of ecstasy never before experienced by humankind, and that whatever happens to me she will be in my heart forever.'

'Good ticket,' said Blotto.

Petrovsky looked towards the opposition group. Yuri Guriakin was waving at him. 'Right, I think it is time we start the duel,' he said.

As was the custom back in the days when duelling had been legal, an independent arbiter had been brought in to run the event. He was an ancient Colonel from a cavalry regiment, whose cheeks above his luxuriant white moustaches were marked with the parallel lines of old duelling scars.

Calling together the two participants, with their seconds, he spelled out the rules. Since he spoke in Russian, Blotto hadn't a wisp of an idea what he was talking about and was grateful for an edited translation from Petrovsky.

'Basically, we stand back to back where he digs his sabre into the ground. On his command we walk ten paces, turn and fire.'

The Colonel then opened a box containing two identical revolvers. They were examined to check that they had not been tampered with and were loaded and ready to fire. Then, as befitted his rank, Prince Evgeni Labatrov was allowed to make the first choice of weapon. Petrovsky, with a look of fatalism, took the remaining pistol.

So that there shouldn't be any bad feeling, the Colonel asked the two men to shake hands before the duel commenced.

'Congratulations on your inevitable victory, Your Highness,' said Petrovsky.

'Bad luck,' said the Prince with an insolent grin. 'Looks like you'll be leaving the field open to me so far as the Lady Honoria Lyminster is concerned.'

Petrovsky made no response.

The Colonel planted his sabre in the ground. The duellists stood back to back. Then, on the word of command, they both started to walk.

Though to say that is not entirely accurate. While Petrovsky took measured paces of equal length, Prince Evgeni Labatrov scampered off like a hunted hare. He had turned and fired his first shot while his opponent was only on his fifth step.

The Prince may have been good at hitting a moving target at five hundred metres, but evidently he wasn't so good at close quarters. Before Petrovsky reached his tenth pace three more shots had been fired at his retreating back. And they'd all missed.

Count Kasimir Petrovsky reached step ten and turned.

He raised his revolver, sighted along the barrel and shot the Heir to the Tsar stone dead.

# 17

# A Wanted Man

The body of Prince Evgeni Labatrov had hardly touched the ground before the group near the Goethe statue were almost surrounded by members of the city police, uniformed and extremely angry. Duelling or any shooting of firearms in a public place were very definitely illegal and they wanted to arrest everyone involved in this breach of the city laws.

It was still not full daylight, and rather misty. In the confusion Count Kasimir Petrovsky managed to slip through the police cordon. Blotto did too, though his escape involved punching two policemen so hard that they fell over. Pity he hadn't had his cricket bat with him, could've sorted them out more effectively with that, he mused as he ran out of the Tiergarten by the Brandenburg Gate.

Two more policemen stood in his way. They shouted something which, though he didn't know the meaning of the individual words, he interpreted correctly as a request to stop. He ignored it and ran straight at them. One was bowled over by another fine punch to the chin while the other unholstered a revolver. Blotto felt the wind of a bullet through his blond thatch of hair as he sought the safety of the Adlon. Once inside he galloped up the stairs to knock on the door of Twinks's suite.

When she opened it, he panted out, 'Rather trodden in the jam spillage this time, I'm afraid, Twinks me old muffin-butterer. Berlin police in full cry after me.'

'I'm not donning my worry-boots about that, Blotters. Much more important – are Kazzy's lungs still puffing in and out like good 'uns?'

'They certainly are.' And he told her the outcome of the duel.

'Oh, that's pure creamy éclair,' she said. 'I'd be right down at the bottom of my boots if Kazzy had been coffinated.'

'Well, I saw him slip the leash and pongle off. Looked like he got away. Mind you, all of the Berlin police force are putting the View Halloo on him as well as me.'

'That's a thought,' said Twinks. 'You shouldn't be larricking about here on the landing. We'd better hide you in my suite.'

Once inside, Blotto removed his overcoat and announced, 'We must work out what we do next.' He frequently said this, though of course what he actually meant was: '*You* must work out what we do next.'

Twinks picked up the cue without comment. 'Yes, well, if you've managed to set yourself up as Dish of the Day for the Berlin peelers we've got to go on tippy-toes. Did you hit any of them?'

'A couple of the stenchers will have rather sore jaws when they come round,' he replied, a little shamefaced. Then, remembering the one at the Brandenburg Gate, 'Oh, three, actually.'

Twinks shook her head with annoyance. 'Blotto, I have mentioned this before. No policeman from any force in the world likes being hit.'

'I know.'

'It makes them extremely ratty. They feel that, if there's any hitting to be done, they should be the boddoes doing it.'

Blotto nodded ruefully.

'So what we really need to do is to get you out of Berlin.'

Blotto cheered up immeasurably. 'You mean go back to Tawcester Towers?'

'Well, I suppose—'

'That's a real bingbopper of an idea! Let's get a message to Corky and we can be out of here within the hour.'

Twinks didn't look as enthused as her brother. 'But we haven't achieved what we came to Berlin to achieve.'

'What?' In the confusion of all that had been happening, Blotto had forgotten the original purpose of their visit. But it came back to him in all its ghastliness. 'Oh, you mean those Bashusky lumps of toad-spawn.'

'You've potted the black there, Blotto me old sidecar. We've failed to palm them off on the Lewinskys so, unless we have some real brain-shudderer of an idea, we're going to have to take the poor old thimbles back to Tawcester Towers – and face the wrath of the Mater.'

'Which is always terrible to behold,' said Blotto.

'But there's also another tick in the teacup,' Twinks went on. 'I don't want to leave Berlin at the moment.'

'Getting a taste for all those sausages, are you?'

'No, you soft-top. I don't want to leave until I've seen Kazzy again.'

'Oh.' Blotto's monosyllable was full of gloom. Though every man who met Twinks fell for her like a dropped catch, it was very rarely that she reciprocated their feelings at any level. And the few occasions when it had happened had always spelled bad news for Blotto. He wasn't exactly jealous of his sister, but he did like to have her full attention, particularly when they were collaborating on a case.

'Maybe, Blotters, just you and Corky should go?'

'What, and leave you here on your ownsome? In Berlin?'

'I'll be as right as a rivet. I can look after myself as well as a nursery nanny.'

Blotto shook his head. 'No, if you stay here, I stay here.' He could be quite firm sometimes.

'Well, I can't leave without seeing Kazzy again,' Twinks repeated. 'And if the police are after you, I don't know how long we can hide you here.'

'Tricky ticket,' said Blotto.

They were interrupted by a knock on the door. Fearing a police investigation, Twinks shoved her brother into the bedroom and told him to hide under the bed.

But when she went to the door, she found only one of the Hotel Adlon's uniformed messenger boys, carrying a letter for her on a silver salver. As soon as she'd read it she went to get Blotto out of his hiding place.

'I've had a letter from Kazzy!' she said excitedly. 'He's fine but he's got to lie low for a while. He says he'll come and find me.'

'Where? Here or in jolly old Blighty?'

'He says, Blotters . . .' she checked the text '"I will find you on whatever remote shore of the world you go to, my love is so strong it will overpower every obstacle until you are back in my arms."'

'What guff,' said Blotto. 'But it's a good turn of the capstan, isn't it?'

'What do you mean?'

'Well, we can go back to Tawcester Towers, can't we? I mean, that's not a "remote shore of the world", is it? It's where you live. He'll find you there as easy as raspberries.'

'Ye-es.' Twinks didn't want to be persuaded by this. She relished the idea of continuing to develop her relationship with Petrovsky in the romantic setting of Berlin. But she couldn't deny that Blotto had a point. 'But if we do pongle off back home, we won't have solved the Bashusky problemette, will we?'

'No.' Blotto sounded gloomy. Then he brightened up for a moment. 'Unless of course they fell off the ferry in the English Channel.'

'Spontaneously or with assistance?'

'Well, nobody would ever know which it was, would they?' The words were spoken rather slyly.

133

Twinks was tempted by the idea, but finally decided that what Blotto was suggesting didn't come quite conform to the strict rules of hospitality with which they had been brought up. 'No, I'm sorry, Blotters. It's a no dodo.'

'Oh, broken biscuits,' he said.


So the decision was made that, having totally failed in their mission to offload the Bashuskys, Blotto and Twinks would take the wretched family back to Tawcester Towers. And face the wrath of the Dowager Duchess.

It was not a conclusion that either of them found cheering. Failure did not usually cloud their sunny outlooks. Indeed in the course of all their adventures this would be the first time it had happened to them.

Twinks went out of the suite to find the Bashuskys. She came back with the troubling news that there was a big police presence in the Adlon foyer. They seemed to know that Blotto was in the building and were either just waiting for him to, as he must at some point, come downstairs. Or they were about to come upstairs and ferret him out.

She had also found out that the Bashuskys had gone out shopping. To the KaDeWe. No doubt to buy a lot of things on the account that she had set up. Twinks, it was decided, would go to the department store to collect them and then prepare for the shameful return to England.

Blotto wrote a note to Corky Froggett, telling him to have the Lagonda outside the front of the hotel in an hour. Twinks said she would deliver it to the chauffeur.

After she had left him alone in her suite Blotto, rather dispiritedly, tried to work out how he was going to leave the Adlon without get picked up by the police. He decided that, as in any situation of mortal peril, he'd feel much better if he had his trusty cricket bat in his hand. So he went back to his own suite to retrieve it.

This may in a sense have been a bad move. The policemen in the foyer had decided that waiting for their quarry to come downstairs could be rather boring, while going upstairs to winkle him out might be a better scheme. And the first logical place to look for him would be his own suite.

So, just at the moment Blotto had extracted his cricket bat from the security of a valise, he was disturbed by the peremptory rapping of knuckles on the door and something incomprehensible shouted in German (something which he – rather cleverly, he thought – deduced might mean: 'Open up!').

He did as instructed and found himself faced by three policemen in smart uniforms and shiny black hats. All three had revolvers in holsters on their belts so, before they had time to use them, he put his bat to good use. A leg sweep caught one of them in the chest and felled him, while a hook to the chin sent the second one flying across the landing. The third policeman, though, grabbed hold of the bat as Blotto thrust it towards his midriff and retained his hold as he was sent hurtling down the stairs. Blotto was going after him to retrieve the precious piece of willow, but he now saw other policemen swarming up towards him.

Rushing back into his suite, Blotto closed and locked the door on the inside, but he knew that would only buy him a few seconds' respite. The other policemen would either have a pass key or they'd smash the door down.

He looked around. The only possible escape route was through the windows. There was no balcony and the windows looked straight out from the back of the building. He raised the sash and sat astride the windowsill.

For a moment he wondered whether he'd be able to take any of his clothes or bags with him, but soon realised he would have to wave them goodbye. Even worse, he was going to be parted from his cricket bat.

He set out along the narrow ledge on the side of the building. It was cold. He wished he'd put on his overcoat, but it was too late for that. He'd left it in Twinks's suite.

135

Edging horizontally along the side of the hotel was fine, but he was on the third floor and soon he'd have to change direction to the vertical. He looked down. The pavement was a long way away and it didn't offer the prospect of a soft landing for anyone meeting it at speed.

The only hope seemed to be offered by a drainpipe at the corner of the building. He reached it and tugged to see if it would take his weight. The cold metal felt wobbly in his hands and not that securely attached to the wall. He wondered whether he should risk it.

The sound of shouting from the room he'd just vacated made up his mind for him. The police were getting closer. There was no alternative. He reached out to grab the drainpipe.

The structure creaked and shuddered as it took his weight, but he managed to half-climb, half-slide down to the next ledge, which marked the top of the hotel's ground floor. Because of the height of the Adlon's public rooms, though, he was still a long way off the ground. He had to rely again on the shaky drainpipe.

Just as he grabbed it for the last part of his descent, the bolts securing the thing to the hotel wall sheared away and Blotto found himself hugging the pipe to him as it threatened to dash him to the hard pavement.

Only for a moment, though. The fixings at the bottom held and slowed his descent as the drainpipe bent like a supple tree branch. He was deposited on the ground with the gentleness that he'd seen elephants on newsreels use their trunks to lower their riders. As he stepped away the drainpipe clattered noisily back against the wall.

It may have been the sound that drew the attention of the policemen in the third floor suite, but suddenly there were a lot of them at the window, shouting meaningless imprecations at him. Time for his escape was tight.

During his perilous descent down the side of the Hotel Adlon Blotto had found his mind working with uncharacteristic efficiency. Serious danger always seemed to release something in his brain that made him more intelligent and decisive.

He'd decided that running away to lose himself in the streets of Berlin was not the best idea since the elasticated sock suspender. He didn't know the geography of the place, whereas the city's policemen most certainly would. They'd pick him up in no time.

But he remembered the old Cossack proverb Count Kasimir Petrovsky had mentioned, the one about the best place to hide being nearest to the searchlight. At the time he'd thought it was a load of guff, but in his current predicament all at once it made a lot of sense. Particularly because the need for him to get out of Berlin and back to Tawcester Towers had suddenly become a lot more urgent.

Where he had landed at the back of the Adlon was conveniently near the entrance to the hotel's underground garages, and Blotto rushed down into them like a hare on skates.

There was no way he was not going to recognise the Lagonda. As he ran towards it, the comforting thought came to him that his precious motor did look a lot better than all the other expensive cars of Europe, side by side in the car park.

When he reached the Lagonda, Blotto knew that his luck was in. Standing beside it, polishing the blue paintwork lovingly, stood Corky Froggett.

There was no time for long explanations. 'The police are after me!' cried Blotto. 'Get some of those jerrycans out of the secret compartment! I've got to hide in there!'

The chauffeur asked no questions. He just said a dutiful 'Yes, Milord' and started transferring the petrol cans from the secret compartment to the Lagonda's dickie.

In a matter of moments he had made enough space for the young master. Blotto snuggled into his niche and Corky closed the lid. He then continued his unhurried polishing of the bodywork.

Blotto had disappeared just in time. Suddenly the garage was full of police, shouting orders, waving guns and flashlights. The scene reminded Corky Froggett so much of his time in the trenches that it was fortunate his gun was safely in the car's glove compartment.

One of the officers spoke English and asked the chauffeur if he had seen the Lord Devereux Lyminster in the last few minutes. Corky denied that he had. The officer then, in no uncertain terms, ordered him to stand back while they searched the Lagonda.

Dutifully, the chauffeur did as he was told. He stood back and watched as a bunch of the policemen went over the car with fine toothcombs.

They could find nothing.

Good craftsmen, the Mafia, thought Corky Froggett approvingly.

## 18

# More Plots and Counterplots

Having driven the Bashuskys to KaDeWe in the Hispano-Suiza, Dmitri Raselov parked the car and went into a small coffee house to pass the time. He was surprised, a few minutes later, to be joined by Fyodor Vlachko.

'How did you know I would be here?' he asked.

'I make it my business to know where everyone is at any given minute. The currency in which I deal is information. I ensure at all times that I have more information than my opponents. This is why I am always so successful.'

'Your success is richly earned, Comrade Vlachko,' said Raselov, who had worked out that flattering his superiors in the Bolshevik government was a shrewd policy.

Vlachko shrugged off the compliment and said airily, 'I know that you have driven the degenerate Bashuskys to shop at KaDeWe where they will no doubt indulge their debased tastes by purchasing various tawdry bourgeois fashion items. I have passed this information on to the Kremlin.'

'Really? Is it so important?' asked Raselov.

'Comrade, everything is important when it concerns the vile enemies of Mother Russia.' Though Fyodor Vlachko was not actually saluting, he spoke as if he were.

'Of course,' Dmitri Raselov agreed. 'Death to the enemies of Bolshevism!'

'Yes. Death to the enemies of Bolshevism!' The spy-master smiled a complacent smile. 'And I may say that programme is going very well, Comrade Raselov. We are exterminating the enemies of Bolshevism at a very satis-factory rate. Soon there will be none left inside Russia.'

'And one day none left outside Russia either?'

'That is, of course, the long-term plan. We are even now working on that plan, to lure the degenerate White Russians back into Mother Russia, where they will be summarily executed. And like all plans of the Bolshevik state, it is a plan that will succeed.'

'That is obvious. When it is being administered by men of your quality, Comrade Vlachko, how can it fail?'

'You are indeed correct, Comrade Raselov. But now I will explain why I have come to find you here. You remember the plan we talked about in the bierkeller?'

'Of course. I remember every word you have ever spoken to me, Comrade Vlachko. Words from you are of inestimable value and to be treasured.'

'Excellent. I am glad to hear that you appreciated your good fortune in being able to listen to me. Well, I have received a telegram this morning from Moscow. They wish to move the schedule forward. They want you to put the plan into action straight away.'

'Today?'

'Exactly, Comrade Raselov.'

'It will be my honour to do this for the glory of the Bolshevik regime and for Mother Russia!' said Dmitri Raselov. And this time he couldn't stop himself from rising to his great height and saluting.


When the Chicago Mafia had designed the secret compart-ment in the Lagonda, comfort had not been at the top of their priority list. In fact they had planned the space for bodies who would have ceased to think about comfort, just as they had ceased to think about everything else when the bullets hit them.

So Blotto did feel rather cramped in the pitch black of his hideaway. There was also a pervasive smell of petrol which he wasn't much enjoying. Though a hidden catch made opening the lid possible from inside the compartment, prudence dictated that he shouldn't try that yet. There might still be Berlin police lurking in the Hotel Adlon garage.

No, he'd wait till Corky Froggett released him. That was the safe option.

While filling in time before they were freed many intrepid heroes might have engaged their minds in remembering past triumphs, planning the next step in their current adventure, or playing word games.

Blotto, by contrast, did none of these things. His mind remained in its habitual state of complete vacuity.


Finding all of the Bashuskys in the huge spaces of the KaDeWe was proving more difficult than Twinks had anticipated. She tracked down the Countess and Masha first. They were, predictably enough, in the Women's Fashions department, spending on her account like there was no tomorrow. It took some time to extricate them as neither of the Russian women felt that they had finished shopping yet. Masha seemed to have lost her urgency to go to Moscow; it had been replaced by an urgency to spend as much of Twinks's money as she possibly could.

Eventually, however, they were persuaded that their first priority now had to be driving back to Tawcester Towers.

The male members of the Bashusky clan proved more elusive. They were not to be seen on the many floors of Menswear and it was only after the Countess mentioned their interest in field sports that Twinks led the way to the Hunting department.

There she was just too late to stop both the Count and Sergei from purchasing very fine hunting rifles with her money, but she did eventually convince them of the need to hurry back to the Hotel Adlon and get their bags packed.

Carrying their extensive KaDeWe purchases, they found the Hispano-Suiza with Dmitri Raselov at its side to greet them. They made room for Twinks for the drive back to the Hotel Adlon. On the way Count Igor Bashusky and Countess Lyudmilla Bashuskaya moaned about the prospect of a return to Tawcester Towers. Their taste of the high life at the Lewinsky mansion had made them rather dismissive of the amenities of the Lyminster family estate.

Masha regressed to moaning about how much she wanted to go back to Moscow.

And Sergei moaned on about his passion for Natasha, saying that he could not possibly leave Berlin and that he would kill himself if he was not able to spend the rest of his life with her.

While Twinks was relieved no longer to be the potential cause for his suicide, she was not otherwise in the cheeriest of moods. The circumstances in which she found herself were very far from larksissimo.

Apart from the immediate aggravation of the Bashuskys' moaning, there was another very major damper on Twinks's customary sparkle.

She and Blotto had totally failed in their mission. Given a bit of time, she had thought she might be able to come up with a solution to the Bashusky problem. But with Blotto now a wanted man in Berlin, such hopes were dashed. They had to get out of the city as soon as possible.

And that meant taking the Bashuskys back home with them. Twinks seethed quietly.

Meanwhile in the front of the car an evil smile played round the lips of Dmitri Raselov, as the Hispano-Suiza executed a neat U-turn before driving on out of the city in an eastward direction.

# 19

# Plans in the Garage

There was a discreet tap on the lid of his hideaway and Blotto froze. Then he heard the reassuring voice of Corky Froggett saying, 'Coast's clear, Milord. I think you can come out now.'

The chauffeur opened the secret compartment and Blotto, rather stiff from his confinement, gingerly lifted himself out. He looked round the shadowy space of the Hotel Adlon car park, relieved at being able to confirm Corky's assertion. There were no police in sight.

He still found himself whispering as he asked the chauffeur, 'Did Twinks find you?'

'Yes, Milord. She told me we would shortly be leaving for home. That's why I was giving the Lagonda a final polish.'

'Good man, Corky.'

'Thank you, Milord. So when are you planning to leave?'

'As soon as the last suitcase buckle's clicked.'

'Excellent, Milord,' said Corky Froggett, enjoying the prospect of leaving a place where his instincts told him to shoot everyone in sight.

'I don't think I should stir too far from here, though,' said Blotto. 'Might still be some of those filth-fingering peelers up in the foyer. Corky, would you be able to bring the luggage down from the two suites without drawing attention to yourself?'

'Of course I would, Milord. Not drawing attention to myself is second nature to me. During that last bout of fisticuffs with the Hun I was commended for my skills in camouflage.'

'You're a Grade A foundation stone, Corky.'

'Thank you, Milord.'

'Then all we have to do is wait for Twinks to come back with the horracious Bashuskys and it's – Tawcester Towers, here we come!'


Twinks, needless to say, was the first to notice that they were not being driven straight back to the Hotel Adlon. From her memorising of the street maps of Berlin she quickly identified the route Dmitri Raselov was taking. He was driving them straight towards the Polish border and perhaps ultimately to Russia.

Never one to keep her opinions to herself, she said straight out, 'This is not the right way.'

'Right way to where?' asked Raselov.

'To the Hotel Adlon.'

'No, we are not going to the Hotel Adlon,' he admitted.

This caused a bit of consternation amongst the Bashuskys, but they were quickly calmed when their driver said, 'In fact, I am driving you to the estate of Zoraya-Bolensk. I have recently received news from Moscow that the authorities are handing back estates that have been confiscated from honest Russian aristocrats. When you return to Zoraya-Bolensk, Count and Countess, you will find all of your old servants reinstated and ready to welcome you back to your rightful home.'

This news was received with huge enthusiasm by all the Bashuskys. Except for Sergei, who knew that he was every minute getting further away from his beloved Natasha Lewinsky. His sister, on the other hand, was ecstatic.

Getting to Moscow from Zoraya-Bolensk was going to be considerably easier than getting there from Tawcester Towers. And her parents went on at great length about the welcome they would receive at their estate from the eternally loyal Vadim Oblonsky and his family.

Twinks, however, whose nose was finely attuned to such things, smelt a very large rat. Her knowledge of Russian politics, augmented by what she had been told by Professor Erasmus Holofernes, made her certain that Dmitri Raselov was lying. The Bashuskys were not being driven back in triumph to the land of their birthright. They were being kidnapped and, once inside Russia, would be handed over to the very untender mercies of the Bolshevik regime and the Cheka.

Her own prospects were not a lot more promising. Action was required, and Twinks was highly skilled and practised at taking action.

Without drawing attention to what she was doing, she slipped her hand into her sequinned reticule. She looked at the thick neck of the giant Raselov in front of her, as her fingers closed around the flexible wire garrotte that she always kept for such contingencies. At its two ends were cylindrical wooden handles like those on a cheese wire.

Twinks knew she could whip the garrotte out of the reticule and have it round Dmitri Raselov's neck in a trice, but she needed to choose her moment. If she did it while the Hispano-Suiza was being driven fast along a busy road there was severe potential danger to the car's passengers. She would wait till Raselov slowed down.

Fortunately, just as she had the thought, he did apply the brakes and bring the car to a halt at the roadside. They were in the outer suburbs of the city, all dilapidated tenement buildings and grubby shops.

Twinks was about to reach forward with her garrotte when the front passenger door was opened from the outside and a man in a peasant smock and a discoloured peaked cap stepped in.

'I thought you would like to meet our escort,' said Dmitri Raselov with a harsh laugh. 'His name is Boris.'

The newcomer laughed too, then pulled a revolver out of his belt and focused it on the passengers in the back of the car.

'Just in case any of you had thoughts of escaping,' said Raselov.

'Why should we want to escape?' asked Count Igor Bashusky. 'We are being taken back to the homeland from which we have been exiled so long.'

'I was thinking more of you trying to escape, Lady Honoria,' said Raselov.

Twinks pushed her garrotte back to the bottom of her reticule. For the time being.


Blotto thought he was probably safe sitting in the front of the Lagonda. He kept an eye open for anyone entering the garage, but nobody came. Except for Corky Froggett, who had to make more than one journey to bring the luggage down from the two suites. He said there were a couple of policemen still in the Adlon foyer, but they showed no interest in him.

Had Twinks been there, she might have thought it rather odd that the police weren't keeping a closer eye on Corky Froggett. After all, he was the missing man's chauffeur and if Devereux Lyminster were planning to escape from Berlin, then Corky could well be involved in his plans.

But Blotto himself had no such suspicions. To him the lack of harassment that Corky encountered was just another example of the good fortune which had been Blotto's birthright. Things would be all right. That was his customary assessment of most situations.

Even the thought of having the wretched Bashuskys in tow could not dampen his excitement at the prospect of very soon being back at his beloved Tawcester Towers. And chewing the fat in his stable with Mephistopheles.

Just wait for Twinks to get back to the Hotel Adlon, and they could soon shake the dust of Berlin off their boots forever.

The wait proved to be much longer than Blotto had expected. Lunchtime passed by and there was no sign of Twinks. Dinnertime too came and went and, although Corky Froggett smuggled some very good Room Service food and drink down to him, Blotto was beginning to get a bit anxious as to the whereabouts of his missing sister. She had gone off fairly early in the morning to find the Bashuskys at the KaDeWe and, although Blotto was aware that women could notoriously lose track of time when they were shopping, Twinks's delay in returning to the Hotel Adlon was beginning to feel excessive.

It was Corky Froggett who after dinner had the bright idea of checking at reception to see if there were any messages for Blotto or Twinks. Back down in the garage, he handed two sealed envelopes across to the young master.

Blotto opened the first and saw that the enclosed letter was signed by Count Kasimir Petrovsky. He read:

*Dear Blotto,*
*I write to inform you that, through my sources in Berlin, I have found out that the Bashusky family have been kidnapped by the Bolsheviks. Dmitri Raselov, who seemed to be a supporter of the White Russian cause, has turned out to be a traitor in the pay of the Reds and an agent for Cheka. He is driving the Bashuskys to Moscow, where their fate is unlikely to be very different to that of Tsar Nicholas II and his family.*

'Hoopee-doopee!' cried Blotto.

'What are you hoopee-dooping about, Milord?' asked Corky.

'I've just received the best news since the setting-up of the feudal system! Oh, I feel as though I am gambolling on

147

camomile lawns! Those four-faced filchers the Bashuskys have been kidnapped!'

'By whom, Milord?'

'Bolshewhatsits. They're going to be taken to Moscow.'

'And do you feel under an obligation to rescue them, Milord?' asked Corky Froggett, always alert to the intriguing prospect of violence.

'No, I do not, by Denzil! We have done everything that a decently bred family can do for the stenchers. If they've managed to get themselves kidnapped in a foreign city, then all obligations are at an end. *Noblesse* no longer has to *oblige*.' A huge grin spread across Blotto's honest features. 'Oh, this is such creamy éclair! As soon as Twinks is here we can pongle back to Tawcester Towers as quick as a doctor's bill.'

There was a silence. Then Corky said, 'Milord, you haven't yet read the second letter.'

'No more I have. You're as sharp as a larcenist's lookout, Corky.'

'Thank you, Milord.'

Blotto ran a finger under the flap of the second letter and pulled out the sheet. 'Oh, this one's from Petrovsky too.'

'Yes, Milord. The reception clerk said that it had been delivered at a later hour than the first communication.'

Blotto read:

*I have just found out, through my sources, that the car being driven to Moscow with the kidnapped Bashuskys also contains your sister Twinks.*

'Oh broken biscuits,' said Blotto. 'In fact, biscuits shattered into a hundred thousand pieces!'

# 20

# A New Heir to the Tsar?

Once he'd escaped the police after the duel in the Tiergarten, Count Kasimir Petrovsky had contacted the underground White Russian network of Berlin, who quickly found him a safe apartment in a mansion block not far from Potsdamer Platz. In this sumptuously well-equipped hideaway staff were on hand to provide drinks, meals and any other services he might require. It was there that he'd received the news of the kidnapping of the Bashuskys and Twinks. And from there that he'd sent the messages to Blotto at the Hotel Adlon.

Petrovsky then set up various meetings, the first of which was with the old orthodox priest Father Kyril Yakhunin. They sat either side of a splendid marble table, on which stood a pot of bitter black coffee and a bottle of cognac, as well as the requisite cups and glasses.

'Well,' said Yakhunin, 'it would appear to any outside observer that you have rather destroyed everything we have been working towards for the past five years.'

'What do you mean?' asked Petrovsky.

'All that we've been planning, to find a focus for White Russian support, to challenge the vile Bolshevik regime in Mother Russia, depended on one thing. Having a credible Heir to the Tsar. Something we had at six o'clock this morning and which – thanks to your clumsiness or perversity – we no longer have.'

'You refer to Prince Evgeni Labatrov?'

'Of course I do, Petrovsky. How many other Heirs to the Tsar do we have?' the old man demanded testily.

'I agree. We have lost Evgeni.' There was no apology in the Count's tone. He spoke with considerable confidence.

'You say we've "lost" him, as if you're referring to a dropped handkerchief. The situation is rather more extreme than that. There's no two ways about it, Petrovsky. We did not "lose" the Prince. You shot him.'

'But did it not occur to you, Father, that I might have had a reason for shooting him?'

The old priest looked bewildered. 'Whatever reason could that be? There can be no reason for spilling more Romanov blood.'

'Did you think,' asked Petrovsky coolly, 'that Prince Evgeni Labatrov was worthy to be Tsar of all the Russias?'

'Since when has worthiness been of any relevance in the lives of monarchs? By that standard very few throughout history would have qualified for the role.'

'Yes, but in these days, measured up against the apparently incorruptible Bolsheviks, our candidate for the Tsardom must be as clean as the driven snow. We do not want any derogatory details about his wicked past to emerge.'

'So, Petrovsky, are you suggesting that Prince Evgeni Labatrov had a wicked past?'

'A wicked past, Father, and a wicked present – until his present ended rather suddenly this morning. Come on, you know that, from the time he was told he was the Heir to the Tsar, the Prince has behaved like the worst kind of playboy. He has drunk and taken drugs to excess, he has treated women like so many dishcloths. He has in fact done everything that Bolshevik propaganda has accused the old Romanov regime of doing.'

The priest shrugged. 'So? It runs in the family.'

'Anyway, all I am saying is that the Prince's appalling moral character was the reason why I killed him.'

'Really?' said Yakhunin drily. 'I thought the reason you killed him was because he was showing too much interest in the Lady Honoria Lyminster.'

'Well, that may have been part of it too,' Count Kasimir Petrovsky conceded.

'But the result of your actions,' Yakhunin went on, 'is that we now have White Russians mobilising their troops on the country's every border, waiting only for a national monarchist hero whom they can rally round – and you have just removed that hero.'

'Only with a view to finding a more heroic one,' said Petrovsky.

'What do you mean? I don't understand what you are talking about.'

'The Prince wasn't up to the job. He wasn't a Romanov either.'

Father Kyril Yakhunin looked very affronted. 'You realise that I have vouched for his legitimacy. I found the proof of Tsar Nicholas's earlier dalliance in Denmark. If you say the Prince was not a Romanov then you are challenging my authority, my respectability, my very integrity.'

'But why did you say that Prince Evgeni Labatrov was a genuine Romanov?'

'I said it because I believed it. I said it because I found the proof of his parentage.'

'Oh.' Petrovsky grinned slyly. 'I thought you said it because of the large number of gold bars that were paid to you by the White Russians for supporting their cause.'

'Well, that may have been part of it too,' Father Kyril Yakhunin conceded.

'Most men have a price,' said the Count. 'I know I do.'

The two men looked at each other across the marble table. In the eyes of both was a new knowingness, touched with an element of respect. Now they were negotiating on level terms.

151

'So,' said the priest, 'where are you going to find your more heroic version of Prince Evgeni Labatrov?'

'I have found him.'

'Really?'

'Yes. It will involve a little more historical finessing on your part.'

'And what do you mean by "historical finessing"?'

'I mean "lying", Father.'

'Are you accusing me of lying?' Yakhunin blustered.

'Yes. And don't play the innocent unworldly priest with me. You've just admitted that you validated Prince Evgeni Labatrov's title claim for a payment of gold bars. You know as well as I do that the story you told about the Tsarevich Nicholas being secretly married in Denmark was sheer fabrication. Now I require you to fabricate another story.'

There was a glint of greed in the old priest's eyes as he said, 'And do I get paid again?'

Petrovsky looked doubtful for a moment. Then he said, 'The White Russians have built up quite a substantial fighting fund for eventualities of this kind. I would not normally contemplate paying for such services, but since it was I who caused the change of plan by killing the Prince, I will say yes. You will get the same number of gold bars as you got for fabricating the first story.'

'But that doesn't take into account inflation,' Yakhunin protested, 'and inflation is getting out of hand here in Berlin.'

'You will get exactly the same number of gold bars as you got for your previous fabrication,' said the Count in a tone so forceful that the priest did not argue.

'So,' he asked, 'was your new Heir to the Tsar also born to a Danish mother?'

'No,' said Petrovsky. Then he seemed to go off at a tangent. 'Do you remember the wedding of George, Duke of York – later to become George V of England – to Mary of Teck . . . ?'

'I do, but I don't see what relevance—'

'All will become clear in a moment. Did you accompany the Imperial Russian party to London for that wedding?'

'I did indeed.'

'Well, I want you to think back to that time.'

'What about it in particular?'

'I want you to remember the minor English aristocratic lady with whom the Tsarevich fell heavily in love.'

'But there was no minor English aristo—'

Count Kasimir Petrovsky overrode him forcibly. 'I said I wanted you to *remember*.'

Yakhunin got the point. 'Ah, yes, I think it's coming back to me . . .'

'Good. You should remember it, because it was you who conducted the secret marriage ceremony between the Tsarevich and that lady.'

'Just as I conducted the secret marriage ceremony between the Tsarevich and Countess Kirsten Jensen-Ibsen of Karlsen?'

'Exactly. I am so glad you understand, Father.'

'I am understanding more and more by the minute, Petrovsky. Yes, it's all coming back to me. I remember how much in love the Tsarevich was with . . . I cannot remember the aristocratic lady's name.'

'Nor can I. And it does not matter for the moment. We can make up a good name for her in time.'

'Very well. So . . . the Tsarevich was secretly married to this lady. In London?'

'Yes. In a Russian Orthodox church. I'm sure we can find the name of a suitable one, where you conducted the ceremony.'

'I'm sure we can, Petrovsky. And then in secret the English aristocratic lady – just like Countess Kirsten Jensen-Ibsen of Karlsen in Denmark – gave birth to a baby boy who is legally the Heir to the Tsar of all the Russias . . . ?'

'That is exactly what happened, Father.'

'And am I to be allowed to know the name of this new heir whose legitimacy I am preparing to validate?'

'Yes. His official title is the Lord Devereux Lyminster. But everyone calls him Blotto.'

# 21

# On the Road Again

Blotto wasn't keen on the idea, but he could see that Corky Froggett had a point. For the young master to be at the wheel of a conspicuous blue Lagonda driving through a city all of whose policeman were on the lookout for him might not have been the most prudent of courses. So it was agreed that Blotto should return to the invisibility of the secret compartment while Corky drove them out of Berlin. This was not only shrewd from the security point of view; it also meant that the chauffeur had his hands full and would not be able to retrieve his revolver from the glove compartment and start shooting his old enemies.

Their plan seemed to have worked. Perhaps the fact that they were leaving so late in the evening made their escape easier. Though there was a large police presence on the city streets, none of them showed any signs of suspicion. Indeed, Corky observed, they seemed positively friendly. He noticed the number of them who saluted the Lagonda on its route. He didn't however notice the sardonic smiles many of the policemen exchanged once the car had gone past.

A couple of hours out of the city, when the busy suburbs had given way to a flat unpeopled plain, Corky thought it was safe to stop on the roadside and release the young master from his temporary incarceration. The chauffeur had been tempted to leave it more than two hours because he did so love driving the Lagonda, but he knew his place and knew that the time had come to offer Blotto the wheel.

Which the young master accepted with great alacrity.

When they'd been driving for a while he said, 'We are sure this is the way to Russia, aren't we, Corky me old kipper-griller?'

'Oh yes, Milord, very definitely.'

'Well, that's a good ticket,' said Blotto. 'Once we get to Russia we should find them easily enough.'

'I believe, Milord, that Russia is quite a big country.'

'Is it, by Denzil? Not bigger than good old Blighty, is it?'

'Considerably so, I have been given to understand, Milord.'

'Well, I'll be jugged like a hare! Bit of a rum baba, isn't it, because you wouldn't expect that to be the case.'

'Why not, Milord?'

'Well, England has produced so many brilliant things . . . you know, like the feudal system and cricket . . . and what has Russia produced?'

'I believe that the Russian equivalent of the feudal system lasted a lot longer than our version, Milord.'

'Well, I bet a groat to a guinea it wasn't as spoffing good as ours. And anyway, that's before we start talking about cricket. You're not going to tell me the Russians invented cricket, are you, Corky?'

'No, Milord.'

'There you are then.'

His point proved, Blotto stepped on the accelerator and the Lagonda flew across the uneven roadways of Eastern Germany towards the Polish border.

But before they reached it, they were aware of another vehicle coming up fast behind them. Instinctively, Blotto pushed the Lagonda to its limits to keep ahead. This wasn't because he was afraid of the pursuers, simply because he didn't like to think any car yet created was faster than his Lagonda.

Eventually, though, the chasing vehicle overtook them, making a loud screeching noise. It then cut across the Lagonda's bows at such a sharp angle that Blotto had to shove on the brakes and skid to an undignified halt on the ragged verge at the roadside.

The pursuing car, now ahead of them, had also stopped. Corky Froggett noticed with glee that it carried Berlin registration plates. He reached eagerly into the glove compartment of the Lagonda. Surely, after such an antisocial bit of driving, he would be justified in shooting any Germans who got out of the car.

Blotto was pretty deeply offended too. So much so that he burst out with, 'The fumacious slugbuckets!' And it was rarely that he resorted to strong language of that sort.

The chauffeur and the young master got out of the Lagonda. Corky Froggett kept the hand with the revolver in it behind his back.

Then the passenger door of the car ahead opened.

And Count Kasimir Petrovsky emerged.

The car's back door opened and the robed and bearded figure of Father Kyril Yakhunin stepped out

'Well, I'll be snickered . . .' said Blotto.

'Sorry, we needed to catch up with you,' said the Count. 'I can help you to find the missing Twinks . . .'

'Oh yes? How?' asked Corky Froggett, so disappointed at not being able to shoot a German that he completely forgot his humble role in society.

'Oh yes? How?' echoed Blotto, unable to think of a better way of saying it.

'I can help you,' said Petrovsky, 'because I am a Russian speaker.'

'Possibly,' said Blotto, thinking he was about to be rather clever. 'But do you speak White Russian or Red Russian?'

The Count laughed, as if this had been a deliberate joke, and rather a good one. 'No,' he said. 'Both sides speak the same language. That is about the only thing we have in common.'

'Both sides also want to control our Mother Russia,' said Father Kyril Yakhunin. 'They have that in common too.'

Petrovsky nodded. 'Yes, of course.'

'One thing I have to ask you, me old flambé pan,' said Blotto, 'is: what is that car you arrived in?'

'One of the new Mercedes-Benz. Six cylinder, supercharged.'

'Ah,' said Blotto.

'Ah,' said Corky Froggett.

Neither of them wanted to admit how impressed they were by any car that could beat the Lagonda in a road race. Particularly when the car in question was made by the Germans.

So Count Kasimir Petrovsky transferred a valise and a couple of hampers from the Mercedes-Benz's dickie to the Lagonda's. Father Kyril Yakhunin also had an extremely heavy bag which he wanted stowed 'somewhere secure'. The obvious destination was the car's secret compartment.

As Corky Froggett took the bag and felt its weight, he said, 'Blimey! What've you got in here – gold bars?'

The priest laughed rather too heartily at the incongruity of that idea. Then he and Petrovsky got into the back seats of the Lagonda.

And neither Blotto nor Corky noticed that the man driving his car, who had promptly turned it round and set off on the return trip to Berlin, was the same Yuri Guriakin who had acted as second to Prince Evgeni Labatrov in the fatal duel.

# 22

# Into the Heart of Russia

Inside the Hispano-Suiza Twinks remained silent, assessing her situation. The Bashuskys were still babbling on about the wonderful things they would do when they reached Zoraya-Bolensk, totally oblivious to the danger of their predicament.

From her encyclopedic knowledge of geography, Twinks reckoned the route they'd take to Moscow would be via Poznan, Warsaw, Bialystok and Minsk. Comparing how long such a drive would take in England, she guessed if they made stops overnight the journey would take at least four days. If they drove continuously, with Raselov and Boris, the man with the revolver, taking turns at the wheel, they might do it in two.

She had some hopes of effecting an escape at the Polish border. After all, it was not many years since Poland had beaten Russia in a ferocious war. Security at border crossings must be tight. And the arrival of a Hispano-Suiza full of Russians – with English number plates – must raise some level of suspicion.

But her hopes were dashed. At the border control nobody even asked for their passports. Dmitri Raselov just handed a bulging brown envelope to the guards and, once the amount it contained had been checked, the Hispano-Suiza was waved through.

Escape was not going to be easy. Although their 'escort' Boris had put away his revolver, Twinks was constantly aware of him watching her. She had thought she might have opportunities to get away if they booked into hotels overnight, but it soon became clear that her captors were going for the continuous driving option. Dmitri Raselov had stocked the Hispano-Suiza's dickie with fairly basic food – bread, cheese and sausages – so they did not even have to stop for meals.

But Twinks was not downhearted. She thrived on adversity. She loved the challenge of finding a way through it. She knew that in time everything would be larksissimo.

In the Lagonda some way behind them the decision had also been taken to drive with the minimum of stops, Blotto and Corky Froggett taking turns at the wheel. The hampers that Count Kasimir Petrovsky had transferred from the Mercedez-Benz turned out to be full of very good food and drink, so they travelled in some style.

Petrovsky clearly knew the protocol at the Polish border. His bulging brown envelope was also checked and found to be satisfactory, and they too were waved through.

There was not much conversation in the Lagonda. Petrovsky and Father Yakhunin had agreed that they would delay telling Blotto that he was now the Heir to the Tsar. They both recognised that his brain worked best when unburdened with too much information.

But there was one thing the two Russians could check out. They had passed Poznan and were approaching Warsaw. Corky was driving, with the young master in the passenger seat beside him. Petrovsky reached into the pocket of his military jacket and produced a false beard of exactly the same colour as Blotto's hair.

'I wonder, old chap,' he said, 'would you try this on?'

'Tickey-tockey,' said Blotto affably. 'Going to have to be in disguise to rescue Twinks, are we?'

'I just feel we should be ready for all eventualities,' was the Count's smooth reply.

'Good ticket,' said Blotto. Pointing to the rear-view mirror, he added, 'You can do without this for a moment, can you, Corky?'

'Certainly, Milord. No worries on a road as straight as this one.'

Blotto hooked the beard over his ears and moved the mirror round so that he could see his reflection. The lower half of his face was now covered with facial hair and dominated by a particularly lavish moustache whose ends curled upwards.

'Well, I'll be spatchcocked like a chicken!' he said. 'I could be a dead ringer for His Majesty George V!'

Blotto was unaware of the looks of delight exchanged between Petrovsky and Yakhunin and they didn't spell out to him the reason for their glee. Because of course George V of England was a cousin of the deceased Tsar Nicholas II of all the Russias, and there had been a strong family likeness between the two men. The fact that even Blotto himself could see it was very good news for the plotters in the back of the Lagonda.


Twinks's estimate of how long the thousand-plus miles from Berlin to Moscow would last had not taken into account the state of the Polish roads. There seemed to be no major thoroughfares. They had to drive through every little village on the route. And though they encountered few motorised vehicles, there were any number of horse-pulled coaches, ox-carts and sledges to scare off the road into the ditches. Progress was painfully slow.

What's more, the further east they got the deeper the temperature plummeted. There were frequent delays when the road ahead had to be cleared of snow. Twinks's optimistic reckonings of the journey being completed in a

161

couple of days now gave way to the recognition that they could be on the road for at least a week.

But being Twinks, of course she did not let such conjectures lower her spirits. She still felt confident that ultimately everything would be larksissimo.

Mind you, she was getting a bit sick of Masha saying how excited she was at the prospect of finally getting back to Moscow, and of Sergei saying, the further he was driven away from Natasha Lewinsky in Berlin, the more likely he was to shoot himself.

Some scores of miles behind the Hispano-Suiza, the group in the Lagonda were also finding their progress slow-going.

Also, once they had crossed the border between Poland and Russia (a passage eased by another stuffed brown envelope handed to the armed guards), Blotto noticed a couple of things that he thought rather odd.

First, once they left the border post, a black car slipped out of a garage there and seemed to be following them. It kept some hundred yards behind, but speeded up and slowed down whenever they did.

'Isn't that a bit of a rum baba?' he said to the Count. 'Is it these Red boddoes keeping an eye on us?'

'No, no,' Petrovsky reassured him. 'It is an escort of White Russians. They are welcoming us to Mother Russia.'

'Tickey-tockey,' said Blotto. 'Decent of them. They're good greengages.'

The Count gave a look to Father Kyril Yakhunin which suggested he might be about to move the conversation on to something more pertinent.

'Blotto,' he said, 'I feel it is time that we talked about the purpose for which we are going to Moscow.'

'Don't don your worry-boots about that. It's as simple as one and one. And if the dice falls on our side, then we may not even have to go as far as that swamp-hole called Moscow.'

'Sorry, I do not understand.'

162

'Well, look, Kasimir me old fish knife, all we're trying to do is rescue Twinks. If we can catch the Hispano-Suiza before we get to Moscow, then the toast will have landed with the butter side up. We just transfer the honoured sibling into the Lag, turn round – and it's full sail and spinnaker for Tawcester Towers!'

'Yes.' This did not quite accord with Petrovsky and Yakhunin's plans for the new Heir to the Tsar. Still, the Count felt confident he could deal with any problems that Blotto might pose. 'Of course, if the Bashuskys do get to Moscow, it's quite possible that your sister will be in as much danger as they are.'

'Oh,' Blotto said airily, 'the noble sis is a Grade A foundation stone when it comes to danger. She laps it up like a kitten does cream. I'm not worrying about her letting the side down.'

'No, I'm sure your confidence is well placed,' said Petrovsky. 'All I wish to say is that, if it does end up that we reach Moscow, you might find you need to speak on your sister's behalf.'

'That's tickey-tockey,' said Blotto. 'If the Bolsheywhatsits try to arrest her, I'd be quite happy to speak up on the poor little droplet's behalf.'

'Yes, I'm sure you would. There is one slight problem that might pose itself . . .'

'And what's that, Petrovsky me old fishing basket?'

'You'd have to speak in Russian.'

'Oh,' said Blotto. 'Yes, that could be a bit of a chock in the cogwheel. Never much of a whale on foreign languages – or on anything foreign, come to that. The beak who taught us French at Eton said he'd never had a muffin-cruncher who had less of a clue. Seven years of French and all I could say was, "Merci."' Blotto grinned. 'Which means "Please".'

'I could teach you what you have to say in Russian,' Petrovsky suggested. 'Phonetically.'

'But we're both in the same car.'

'I am sorry?'

'Well, so it seems a bit daft to teach me by telephone.'

'No,' said Petrovsky. 'Listen, we have this long journey with nothing to do. Plenty of time for you to learn a speech in Russian. Father Kyril will help too, won't you, Father?'

'Of course.'

And so Blotto was launched on to the process of learning a speech in Russian.

Broken biscuits, he thought to himself miserably. This is worse than being back in a classroom at Eton.

He looked in the rear-view mirror. There were now three black cars following the Lagonda.

# 23

# Red Square

By the time the Lagonda finally reached Moscow, the escort it had gathered behind amounted to perhaps twenty vehicles. As well as more black saloons, there were also armoured cars. 'To welcome us,' Count Kasimir Petrovsky kept reassuring Blotto. 'Things have changed so much in Russia in recent years. They are very pleased to welcome foreign visitors – particularly from a friendly country like England.'

And each time he was told this, Blotto said, 'Good ticket' and continued trying to memorise the Russian speech that Petrovsky was so insistent he should learn. He was now very keen to get it right. Until he knew its content he had had the same attitude towards it as he had to school home-work. But once the Count had told him it was in fact a plea for the entire Russian nation to take up cricket and an explanation of the rules, Blotto was determined to become word-perfect.

The roads in Russia were worse than those in Poland, and as they progressed further east the temperature fell and the thickness of the frozen snow increased. But thanks to the solid British engineering of the Lagonda – and to the great satisfaction of Blotto and Corky Froggett – they suffered no breakdowns.

Once they reached the outskirts of Moscow, more than a week since they had left Berlin, Petrovsky gave directions through the narrow streets of the capital. Blotto felt even more cheerful than ever, confident that he would soon be reunited with Twinks. Then it'd be – turn the Lagonda round and full speed ahead to Tawcester Towers.

He couldn't help noticing that there were a lot of armed police and soldiers on the streets. They took great interest in the Lagonda-led convoy, but their faces remained grim to the point of being hostile.

'Thought they might give us the odd wave, Kasimir,' said Blotto. 'If, as you say, they're now making English visitors welcome.'

'Ah,' the Count explained. 'Regulations under the new regime do not allow them to wave – or even to smile – but they are extremely pleased to see you.'

'Good ticket,' said Blotto.


The drive through the dark dank streets of Moscow might have dispirited a less resilient soul than Blotto's, but his customary optimism had been bolstered by Petrovsky's words and he was cheered by the thought of soon seeing his sister. Also, as they drew nearer their destination with Corky Froggett at the wheel, the clouds cleared, the heavy snow was subdued into a fairytale powdering and a white orb of sun glowed in a patch of cold blue sky.

It had never occurred to Blotto that he might have any difficulty in finding his sister. He was vaguely aware that, if it came to searching for her, there was quite a lot of Russia to search. But he felt confident that Petrovsky knew where he was going and would direct the Lagonda straight to where Twinks would be found.

And so it proved. The Count directed Corky to drive into the middle of Red Square and there to stop. On all sides there was a huge police and military presence, armed to the teeth and bearing red flags decorated with hammers and sickles, but as the passengers emerged from the Lagonda nobody moved.

Blotto felt the sharpness of the icy temperature as he stretched his weary limbs. He looked around with some amazement at the exotic architecture that surrounded him.

Then he felt the impact of something soft, damp and very cold on the back of his neck. He turned to see Twinks standing there with the mischievous, guilty look of someone who has just thrown a snowball.

Some brothers and sisters, reunited after a time of danger and uncertainty, might have rushed into each other's arms. But that wasn't the way Blotto and Twinks had been brought up. They did come from the English upper classes, after all.

So, instead of hugging each other, Twinks simply said, 'How're your trousers holding up, Blotto me old tinder-box?'

And Blotto said, 'Snubbins to you, Twinks me old dressing-gown cord!'

In this way was communication between the two siblings re-established.

Blotto next became aware that behind Twinks stood the entire Bashusky family. He also noticed the Tawcester Towers Hispano-Suiza on the front of whose bonnet a small flag now fluttered. The flag was red with a black hammer and sickle on it.

He had just observed this when the massed soldiers around Red Square came to life and arrested everybody.

# A Fair Trial?

When she heard of their destination, Twinks of course knew and Blotto of course didn't know about the evil reputation of Moscow's Butyrka Prison. She was aware of its past as a transit post for criminals on their way to internal exile in such destinations as Siberia. She had heard of its more recent usage as a hellhole into which enemies of the Bolshevik regime were packed like doomed sardines, and from which prisoners only emerged to face firing squads. But she didn't see any point in casting a cloud over her brother's sunny disposition by mentioning any of this.

Twinks observed in the very crowded Hispano-Suiza which took them rattling from Red Square to Butyrka Prison that, apart from herself, Blotto and Corky Froggett, the only other people in the car were the Bashusky family. She had not expected Dmitri Raselov and his henchman Boris to be taken into custody, but she had seen Bolshevik soldiers laying hands on Count Kasimir Petrovsky and Father Kyril Yakhunin. Presumably they were in another vehicle or being incarcerated somewhere else.

Twinks fortunately still had her sequinned reticule, containing the garrotte and various other useful instruments of mayhem, but she felt disinclined to use any of them. There were too many guards in the van for an effective coup to be engineered at that point. She decided to bide her time and see what the future brought.

Twinks looked across at her brother, hoping he wasn't letting the seriousness of their situation get him down.

She needn't have worried. There was a boyish gleam of excitement in Blotto's eye as he said, 'And do you know, Twinks me old switch-clicker, the final dollop of butter on top of the crumpet is that I'm going to help introduce cricket into Russia!'

She didn't have time to comment because at that point the Hispano-Suiza came to a halt directly outside the prison gates.

Once inside Butyrka, Twinks had expected that they would be separated by gender, but in fact they were all shoved together into a noisome holding cell where fluids that didn't bear too much investigation ran down the walls and over the floor. The metal door clanged shut behind them. Inside Butyrka Prison everything seemed to clang.

To her surprise, the Bashuskys seemed to be as cheerful as Blotto about their circumstances. Even after spending more than a week in the company of Dmitri Raselov and Boris, the Count and Countess remained convinced that their precious estate of Zoraya-Bolensk was about to be returned to them, and that they would be welcomed there by Vadim Oblonsky.

Masha was ecstatic that she had finally got back to Moscow, and apparently unaware that she wasn't seeing the best of it. Only Sergei still seemed upset, threatening yet again to shoot himself because he was so far away from Natasha Lewinsky.

So, apart from him, Twinks had to do all the worrying. And she was a little worried as to the fate that was being planned for them by the Bolshevik authorities. She wondered if they were all doomed just to be forgotten, to waste away unseen in Butyrka Prison.

* * *

169

But it soon seemed that this was not going to be the case. Within an hour of their arrival, they were bustled out of the holding cell by armed guards and taken along endless dank corridors, through many metal doors that clanged shut behind them, to what appeared to be a courtroom.

At one end was a long table with three chairs behind it. Two were occupied by grim-looking men, while the centre one was empty, waiting perhaps for the senior judge. The two men who were there wore peasant smocks and peaked caps. In the view of Twinks, the fact that they wore hats indoors said everything that needed to be said about their breeding – or rather lack of it.

The prisoners were herded into a pen facing the long table with as little care as if they had been farmyard beasts. And the guards kept their rifles pointed at them. A sullen obstinacy in the men's eyes showed they would have no compunction about shooting if the necessity arose (or even if it didn't). Twinks was unsurprised to find that there was no jury box in the courtroom.

In spite of the grimness of their situation, the Bashuskys' optimism remained undented. 'You wait,' said the Count. 'Very soon Vadim Oblonsky will arrive to take us to Zoraya-Bolensk.' Twinks shook her head with pity for his complete misunderstanding of their predicament.

A door in the wall behind the judges' table clanged open.

A small Lenin-capped man with a moustache and a beard which only covered the point of his chin appeared and took the empty central seat. The door clanged shut.

Count Igor Bashusky could not contain his excitement.

'See, I told you!' he cried. 'This is Vadim Oblonsky!'

# 25

# The Sentence of the Court

'I am not Vadim Oblonsky any more,' said the chief of the judges, who had heard the Count's words. 'Like our illustrious leader of sacred memory, who changed his name from Vladimir Ilyich Ulyanov to Lenin, I have changed mine from Vadim Oblonsky to Fyodor Vlachko.'

Blotto and Corky Froggett hadn't a clue what was going on because the man spoke in Russian. But Twinks understood, and so did the Bashuskys. Nevertheless it was a long way into Vlachko's diatribe before the optimistic smile was finally wiped off Count Igor's face.

It wasn't only the change of name that Fyodor Vlachko had copied from Lenin, he also modelled his oratory on the great leader's lengthy and hectoring manner. It was more than an hour into his denunciation of White Russian principles in general when he moved to the specifics of the life he had led at Zoraya-Bolensk.

'. . . and the appalling way we were treated by the family who owned the house – who owned it not because they had earned the right to own it by the sweat of their brows, but simply by accident of birth. The Bashuskys represented everything that was corrupt and contemptible about the despicable Romanov regime. They treated me and my family worse than they treated their dogs. They shouted orders at us all the time, often they beat us when we did not do exactly what they demanded. Comrades, it is wonderful that I have managed to arrange for these evil degenerates to be brought back to Mother Russia to face this tribunal and to ensure that justice is finally done!

'I wish there was a worse sentence I could impose for the crimes against the honest workers of Russia by generations of evil Bashuskys, but sadly death is the maximum allowable.

'It is therefore the legal finding of this court, having heard all the evidence . . .'

But there hasn't been any spoffing evidence, thought Twinks.

'. . . that all of the accused standing in front of us are, by a majority verdict . . .' He looked fiercely at his co-judges, who didn't want to get on the wrong side of Comrade Vlachko and hastily nodded agreement. '. . . sentenced to be killed by firing squad!'

All four Bashuskys looked poleaxed by shock, but there was a point that Twinks thought worth making. In fluent Russian she said, 'Look, that may be all very jolly and grandissimo for the Bashuskys, but what you don't seem to have twigged, me old fly-swatter, is that there are three people in this dock who have absolutely nothing to do with the Bashuskys.' She didn't think it was the moment to point out that she and Blotto were actually distant cousins of the family. 'What's more, we have the great honour to be something which I'm sure you would have given your last baby tooth to have been born as – British citizens! We have committed no crimes and therefore cannot be sentenced to any punishment. And because we actually come out of the top ranks of British society, anything unpleasant that happens to us will be taken very seriously by His Majesty's government. So you condemn us at your peril. You risk triggering an international incident. You touch one hair of our heads and Britain will send several gunboats!'

Fyodor Vlachko looked unimpressed by Twinks's oratory. After a very brief whispered consultation with his two fellow judges, he announced, 'No, a person of my eminence cannot be sidetracked by minor details of status and nationality. It'll be simpler if you all face the firing squad. Guards, take them back to their cells to await execution!'

For the first time Masha Bashuskaya was less than convinced that she wanted to be back in Moscow.

# 26

# On Death Row

After passing through many clanging metal doors, the final metal door clanged shut behind them and they were back in the holding cell where they'd started, still surrounded by guards. The Bashuskys, who might now be thought to have something serious to moan about, had been strangely silent on the way back from the courtroom.

They were hardly inside the cell before the door was flung open again with considerable force to admit a very red-faced and angry-looking guards officer. He immediately began to bawl out the leader of the guards who had escorted them.

Twinks of course understood every word he said. 'You idiot!' he shouted at the hapless guard. 'I've just received the printed order from the courtroom. You weren't meant to bring the prisoners back here. For God's sake, you should have heard the sentence. They should be taken to death row! Sort it out immediately!'

And he bustled out, clanging the door shut behind him with considerable force.

The prisoners who hadn't understood the recent exchange – in other words, Blotto and Corky Froggett – had the change of accommodation explained to them as the entire group were hustled out of the holding cell, with the door clanging shut behind them.

They were led down more corridors, through more clanging doors, until another cell was opened and the Bashuskys were unceremoniously ushered into it. Then the door clanged shut on them. There was no opportunity for good-byes, and Twinks reckoned, with a modicum of sympathy, that the chances of their ever meeting again made backing a snail in the Grand National look like a good bet.

As they led the English party to their destination, the guard who had been bawled out by the officer moaned to his colleague (there were just the two of them now). He little realised that Twinks could understand every word he said.

'Way out of order, I'd say, him shouting at me like that. Behaving like a tin-pot dictator and he used to be a serf whose job was mucking out the stables. I know it's not a popular thing to say these days, Leonid – possibly even a dangerous thing to say – but I don't think all of the recent changes in this country have been for the good.'

'You can say that again, Ivan. And, as you know, your secret's safe with me.'

'Yes. I'm not against the principle of what's happened, Leonid . . . you know, the idea of more equality and what-have-you, but it doesn't seem to have worked out that way. The people running the country now seem just as corrupt and greedy as the lot they got rid of.'

'You've put your finger on it there, Ivan.'

'With the bunch of tossers we've got now, I often think the old Romanovs weren't so bad. I'm not sure topping the lot of them was maybe such a clever idea after all. I tell you, Leonid, if it turned out there was an Heir to the Tsar still alive and he come in here, I'd welcome him with open arms . . . yeah, and do anything to help him get back in charge. Somehow, having the country run by toffs feels right, in a way that it being run people who used to muck out stables doesn't.'

'Well, this is it, Ivan,' said his mate.

Twinks found the exchange interesting, but wasn't too optimistic of encountering many other Russians who shared Ivan and Leonid's views.


Once the guards had left them on their own, Corky Froggett started yawning, though he kept trying to hide the fact behind his hand.

'Oh, look, Corky,' said Twinks, gesturing to one of the grubby paillasses on the damp floor, 'why don't you take the weight off the old sock-stretchers? You did so much of the driving, your horse power must be down to a toy pony. Shut the peepers for a while.'

'I'm not sure that I can do that, Milady.'

'Why on earth not?'

'I'm not sure that it's appropriate for someone of my humble station in life to sleep at a time when the young master and the young mistress are still awake.'

'Oh, don't talk such toffee, Corky! You just curl up like a woodlouse and waft off on the waves of oblivion.'

'If you're sure, Milady, that I am not overstepping the—'

'I'm as sure as a mother-in-law's opinion. You agree too, don't you, Blotto?'

'Tickey-tockey.'

Soon, although he lay down rigidly at attention, Corky was asleep. From the mouth beneath his bristling white moustache a regular snore rather like sea-wash emanated.

'Well,' said Twinks, uncharacteristically gloomy, 'in a rather deep glue pot now, aren't we, Blotto me old fish-gutter?'

'What do you mean, Twinks me old collar stud?'

'Small business of facing the firing squad . . .'

'Oh, that,' said Blotto dismissively. 'Don't don your worry-boots about that.'

'I'm not quite sure how we're going to get out of it.'

'Well, we'll escape, won't we? We always spoffing well escape, don't we?'

'Ye-es,' said Twinks, less totally convinced than she normally was. She looked around the suppurating grey walls of their dark cell without enthusiasm. On the forbidding stone slabs former inmates had scrawled messages of despair. At least, she thought, the words were in Russian so there was no danger of their depressing her brother.

Not that Blotto appeared in any danger of being depressed. If it was possible he seemed more perky than usual. 'We'll get out of this treacle tin just as we have out of every other one,' he asserted. 'We're not just your average tadpoles, are we? We are Blotto and Twinks, after all.'

'Yes,' his sister agreed, trying not to reveal how negative she felt. 'Can you see any obvious way of escape from here then?'

Blotto's pure-blue eyes scanned the solid walls and equally solid metal door of their cell. 'Well, not an obvious way, no,' he admitted. 'But some real buzzbanger of an idea will come to us very soon, as sure as eggs are round.'

'But eggs aren't round,' said Twinks. 'They're oval.'

'Yes. Bad example,' Blotto agreed. 'But we'll get out of this clammy corner, don't you worry.'

'And if we don't?'

'If we don't, we'll still have had a nice fruity innings. We've had some larks, haven't we, Twinks?'

'Oh, it's all been absolutely larksissimo.'

'And if we're due to be stumped so early in the game . . . well, tough Gorgonzola.' This was as near as Blotto ever got to being philosophical. 'I mean, the way I see it is . . . most of the time life's pretty crumpety and then every now and then bits of it are really the flea's armpit, but when you look back you only remember the crumpety bits. So yo-ho-ho and hoopee-doopee!'

In some religions there are deeply meaningful quotations from sacred texts, prayers and mantras. But for Blotto everything he believed in could be summed up in that phrase. 'Yo-ho-ho and hoopee-doopee!'

There was a silence, then Twinks said, 'I wish they'd given us a bat's squeak of an idea about timing.'

'Timing?'

'You know, when they're going to take us out to . . . you know . . .'

'Oh right, good ticket.'

'I don't think in these kind of situations the Bolsheviks usually hang around to powder their noses.'

'Like to get to the bully off early, do they?'

'Yes.' Twinks grimaced, though even a grimace couldn't make her face look less than beautiful. 'So the next person who comes through that door, Blotto me old back-scratcher, could be one of the last people we ever see.'

'Alternatively, Twinks me old cucumber frame, it could be someone come to rescue us.'

Twinks grinned. It was hard not to grin when her brother said things like that, however unlikely they might be. Yes, she reflected, her life had been pretty crumpety. And it would have been much less crumpety if she hadn't had Blotto to share it with.

There was a clang from outside as a huge key was thrust into the lock of their cell. Then another clang as the door was thrust open. Brother and sister tensed as they looked towards the source of the noise.

In the doorway stood Count Kasimir Petrovsky.

'Hello,' he said. 'I have come to rescue you.'

## 27

# To St Petersburg!

'There is one good thing to have come out of your visit to Moscow,' said Petrovsky.

'What is that?' asked Twinks.

'You have achieved what you wanted to achieve.'

'Sorry, Kazzy? I haven't got a midge's buzz of an idea what you are talking about.'

'You came to Berlin to get rid of the Bashusky family.' The Count shrugged and spread his arms wide. 'So? You have got rid of the Bashusky family.'

It was true, but neither Twinks nor Blotto felt any urge to celebrate the fact.

They were in the Lagonda, Corky Froggett driving. Blotto sat in the passenger seat, with Twinks and Petrovsky in the back. The couple's mutual ardour had not cooled, but they managed to keep their hands off each other. Both had the feeling that another major hazard lay ahead. Once they'd negotiated that, then there would be time for passion.

Besides, Father Kyril Yakhunin was sitting on the back seat between them.

Like the Hispano-Suiza they had seen in Red Square, the Lagonda's bonnet now carried a red hammer and sickle flag. Both Blotto and Corky Froggett had protested when they first saw it spoiling the beauty of their precious car, but Petrovsky had convinced them of the necessity of leaving it there. Cars with that emblem were only driven by the most senior members of the Bolshevik government. No police or soldiers would attempt to stop a car carrying the flag. It would give them free, unimpeded passage anywhere in Russia.

Petrovsky had told them their destination was St Petersburg. (Like all White Russians, he would have no truck with this ridiculous new naming of the imperial city. It would never be Petrograd or Leningrad, but always St Petersburg to him.) He had, however, been vague about the precise nature of their mission once they arrived there. He had insisted that Blotto put on the false beard he had tried earlier, and also that he ran through the lines of the speech he had been asked to memorise. When Blotto asked if he should practise out loud, Petrovsky said no.

Twinks, alert as ever, was intrigued. Though she was in love with the Count, the suspicion came to her that he, aware of her knowledge of Russian, did not want her to hear the content of Blotto's speech. But, even if that were the case, she had no doubt that he was acting in the best interests of all of them.

'Can I just get this right, Kasimir me old greengage?' said Blotto. 'Once I've done this little job for you in St Petersburg, that's it. I'll be stood down from action, will I? And we can all go pongling back to good old Tawcester Towers?'

'That is it,' the count replied. 'You are exactly right. Once you have done that "little job" for me, you will be as free as the birds in the air. Though . . .' He looked soulfully at Twinks through the fuzz of Father Yakhunin's beard '. . . I hope that your sister will not have to go straight back to England. I hope that she and I will be able to enjoy some moments of bliss together in Berlin.'

'That would be grandissimo,' said Twinks.

*　*　*

Though Corky Froggett and Blotto once again shared the burden and drove through the night, the five hundred miles between Moscow and St Petersburg was slow-going, with the usual hazards of horse-drawn vehicles, ox-carts and sledges to frighten into the ditches. But what Count Kasimir Petrovsky had said was borne out. The red flag flying on the Lagonda's bonnet ensured they received no interference from the authorities. Indeed, when they passed police control posts and roadblocks, barriers were immediately raised and the officers even saluted them.

Twinks hardly dared to think how useful this immunity would be when they finally were on their way out of Russia. She knew a lot of dangers would have to be survived before they reached that point.

# 28

# The Heir to the Tsar Speaks!

It was about nine o'clock in the evening when they reached the outskirts of St Petersburg. Twinks, who had read a lot about the fabled city, was disappointed in what she could see of it illuminated in the Lagonda's headlights. Everything looked utterly run down and depressed, grey and dispirited.

Blotto was driving the last leg, and Count Kasimir Petrovsky gave him detailed instructions of how to reach their destination. He was ordered to stop outside what had once been a mansion block but now looked more like a tenement block. Petrovsky said they should take anything they might need for an overnight stay out of the dickie.

'And will it be all right if the car's just left here on the street?' asked Corky Froggett. He had seen dark figures lurking in the shadows as they drove through the city and he didn't want anything unpleasant to happen to the precious Lagonda.

'Yes, that is a good point,' said Father Kyril Yakhunin in Russian. 'I have certain valuables in the car which I would not wish to be purloined.'

'Have no worries on that score,' said the Count, again in Russian. 'That flag would keep the Lagonda safe in the headquarters of the most vicious gang in the entire country.

No one wants to get on the wrong side of the Bolshevik authorities. It'd be more than their lives are worth.'

Twinks translated this cheering news to Blotto and Corky.

Though the exterior of the block had been so unpromising, the apartment into which Petrovsky led them was luxuriously appointed.

'Where are we, actually?' asked Twinks.

'This is a safe house for Bolshevik dignitaries,' the Count replied.

'But surely you're not a Bolshevik dignitary. You are a White Russian.'

'Yes. But I arrived in a car with a Bolshevik flag on it. Nobody will think to check my credentials until tomorrow morning at the earliest. And by then this apartment will have served its purpose and we'll be out of it.'

'Can you tell me what's going to happen tomorrow?' asked Twinks plaintively. 'It's clearly going to be a major fireworks display.'

'It certainly is, my love. But I am afraid I cannot tell you. In today's Russia you cannot trust anyone.'

So Twinks had to be content with that. She didn't press for more. Something in Petrovsky's expression told her that the following day would witness a momentous event in the history of post-revolutionary Russia.

Her brother looked rather uncomfortable, standing there aimlessly, no doubt wishing he had his cricket bat with him, to hold and give him a sense of purpose. 'I say, Kasimir me old tea tray,' he said, 'can I take this fumacious beard off now? It's itching against my stubble like a burr in a bathing suit.'

'You may take it off overnight, but tomorrow you must wear it. You must also before you go to sleep check through the script that you have learnt. Tomorrow you must be word-perfect.'

'I will be,' said Blotto. 'I know how important it is for these poor Russian pineapples to learn how to play cricket. Once they've done that, they'll forget about all this revolutionary business and start to behave like proper Englishmen.'

'Yes, of course,' said Petrovsky, exchanging a small smile with Father Kyril Yakhunin.

'Are you sure it wouldn't help,' Twinks suggested casually, 'if I were to listen to old Blotters' lines to make sure he's word-perfect?'

But once again Petrovsky vetoed the idea. Twinks wondered if she might somehow get a chance to filch his script for the next day from her brother, but she didn't think the chances were good. The Count and the priest were watching their every movement.

After a meal of caviar, pickled salmon and rye bread, washed down by a great deal of vodka, Petrovsky announced that they should all go to bed. In separate rooms. After Blotto had entered his, the key was turned in the lock from the outside.

As Count Kasimir Petrovsky led Twinks to her room she turned the full power of her exquisite azure eyes on him and said, 'Are you really not going to tell me what is going on?'

'I am sorry,' he replied. 'It hurts me more than I can say to have any secrets from the most beautiful woman I have ever encountered, the one to whom I will be true for the rest of my days, but that is how it must be, for the time being at least. Rest assured, though, that what is being done is for the good of Mother Russia. Tomorrow is a day that will go down in history. Tomorrow will be a day of triumph for the White Russian cause!'

But more details he refused to give her. As they reached her bedroom he kissed her chastely on the lips. 'After tomorrow,' he announced, 'we will have the rest of our lives to express the grandeur and glory of our love!'

Once Twinks was installed in her room and the door was closed, she heard it, like Blotto's, being locked from the outside.

There was nothing she could do but wait to see what the next day would bring.


The Winter Palace of St Petersburg had not yet fully recovered from the attacks and looting that it had suffered during the frenzy of the revolution. Its once splendid façade was pitted and pockmarked from artillery fire. But it still looked impressive, from sheer size alone, and remained a powerful symbol of the imperial power of the Romanovs.

Count Kasimir Petrovsky did not drive there with them the following morning. He said mysteriously that he had other things to arrange. So Corky Froggett, directed by Father Kyril Yakhunin in the passenger seat, drove them through the icy streets of St Petersburg to the huge parade ground in front of the Winter Palace. Blotto and Twinks sat in the back of the Lagonda.

They had been surprised that morning to be told by Petrovsky that they had to dress up in special costumes for the day's proceedings. Twinks was presented with a long black dress to be worn under a long black coat, and a black fur hat with a thick black veil to cover her face.

Blotto, on the other hand, was given a full military uniform, garlanded by an excess of gold braid and elaborate frogging. With the false beard in place over his newly shaved chin, Twinks could not help noticing how like a younger version of the King of England he looked. Wild conjectures as to what Petrovsky was plotting ran through her mind. But again she could only wait to see how events turned out.

When the Lagonda arrived in front of the Winter Palace the parade ground was already full. A huge crowd of uniformed soldiers, policemen and ordinary citizens had gathered. They looked sullen and threatening. All faced a cordoned-off space in front of the Palace's main doors.

Twinks felt that she and her brother were facing certain death. Except there were no guns pointing at them. The only things pointing at them were bulky film cameras on tripods. And huge microphones on stands.

When the Lagonda came to a halt there was a brief altercation between Blotto and Father Kyril Yakhunin. Blotto wondered whether the priest could find a cricket bat for him. 'After all, the poor greengages have probably never seen one. And if I'm talking to them about how to play the game they should be able to clap their peepers on a bit of the kit.'

But the Orthodox priest was adamant that no such object could be found in Russia, least of all in the parade ground in front St Petersburg's Winter Palace. Since his English was limited, Twinks had to translate his words for Blotto's benefit. 'The crowd would find it very odd if you were carrying a bat. They might think it was a weapon. There will be plenty of time for them to learn the fine details of the game later.'

Blotto wasn't pleased, but reluctantly accepted that he'd have to do his demonstration without a bat, and stepped out of the Lagonda.

Twinks was uncertain what she had expected to happen next, but it certainly wasn't what actually did. The minute the crowd saw Blotto, they burst into loud and enthusiastic cheering. Telling Corky to stay at the wheel 'in case we need to make a quick getaway', she slipped out of the car and melted imperceptibly into the throng. She moved forward as Father Yakhunin led her brother to the space in front of the Palace doors.

The priest raised his hands for silence, and checked with the camera- and sound men that their equipment was running. He waited in front of the microphone, arms still upraised, but it was a long time before the rapturous excitement of the throng could be stilled. Eventually Yakhunin was able to make himself heard.

'Citizens of Imperial Russia,' he cried (in Russian of course), 'today is a wonderful day in the history of our glorious country! Because today the Russian people are meeting for the first time the true and rightful Heir to the Tsar of all the Russias!'

He then proceeded to give a potted version of the story he and Petrovsky had devised, about Tsar Nicholas's marriage (while he was still the Tsarevich) to the lady of the English court (for whom he had now invented a name). He told how he had conducted the ceremony in a Russian Orthodox church in London (for which he had researched a name). And with each revelation the cheers of the crowd increased in volume and intensity.

'But now,' he announced, 'you will hear from the man himself – the one who will soon be known as our rightful ruler – Tsar Nicholas III!' And Yakhunin slipped away into the crowd.

Blotto, though having understood nothing else of what the bearded priest had said, had been forewarned that this was his cue, and he stepped up to the microphone with great relish. He was after all about to do a really good act, something that would benefit all of the Russian millions. How could their lives fail to be better once they started to play cricket?

'People of Russia,' he parroted from the text he had so laboriously learned, 'I speak to you as the only rightful ruler of your country. I am the legitimate heir to the late Tsar Nicholas II and soon, with your help, I will be back in this Winter Palace, reigning over you all with benign benevolence! That is what you want me to do, is it not?'

The ecstatic cries of 'Da!' were so loud that it was a while before Blotto could make himself heard again. Twinks had edged her way forward and now stood very near to the cordon around the cameras and microphones. She noticed something familiar about the back-view of a short man standing in front of her, right next to Father Yakhunin.

187

And when she heard him speak, she was amazed to recognise Fyodor Vlachko!

'It is going very well,' he said to the priest. 'Exactly as we planned.'

'Yes,' Yakhunin agreed. 'And all the international press are here?'

'Of course. There is a correspondent from *The Times* of London, from *The New York Times*, *Le Figaro* from Paris and many others. Within hours this story will be reverberating around the world.'

'And then when the film is ready to be shown . . .'

Fyodor Vlachko chuckled. 'Yes, every White Russian will think that they can return safely from their exile.' He pointed toward the figure in the uniform of the Tsar. 'Listen to him.'

Blotto was concentrating like mad to keep getting the words right. He reckoned he'd probably got to the bit of his speech where he was describing the shots available to a batsman in cricket, so he reinforced his words with gestures demonstrating the leg glance and the cover drive. Each of these movements prompted renewed cheering.

'People of Russia,' he continued, 'know that all the changes of the last few years will be reversed. The serfs will give up all ideas of governing the country and will return – with enormous relief – to work on their masters' estates! They will once again know their proper place in the social hierarchy. All the land seized from the aristocrats will be returned to them! So any member of the upper classes who has gone into exile can safely return to their Mother Russia in the secure knowledge that they will receive as warm a welcome as the one I am receiving here today in St Petersburg!'

The reaction which greeted this was even more fulsome than any that had been heard before. Blotto paused until he could again make himself heard.

'And when they do come here, all of the White

Russians . . . ?' Twinks heard Father Kyril Yakhunin say to Fyodor Vlachko.

'We will be waiting for them,' said the former Vadim Oblonsky. 'Our troops of the Red Army are already massing on the borders. We will destroy even more returning White Russians than we killed in the Civil War! And our revenge will be complete!'

Twinks could hardly restrain her indignation at this appalling deception. The thought that her brother was being used as an unwitting pawn in the scheme only made it more reprehensible.

In front of her the Bolshevik and the priest were also discussing Blotto. 'And what will happen to *the Heir to the Tsar*?' asked Yakhunin, putting a particularly snide intonation on to the last words.

'As soon as he has finished his speech and the filming has been completed, he will be liquidated,' said Fyodor Vlachko.

'I would advise you to liquidate his sister at the same time,' said the priest. 'She is a troublesome minx.'

'I will see that it is done.'

'It does not pay to get on the wrong side of Fyodor Vlachko, does it, Comrade?'

'No, it certainly does not.' The revolutionary chuckled.

'So you have already liquidated the Bashuskys, and next you will—'

'No,' Vlachko interrupted. 'The Bashuskys are still alive.'

'Oh?'

'I had to travel here to Leningrad before I could arrange their execution. So I have delayed the firing squad until I return to Moscow.' Fyodor Vlachko chuckled again. It was not a pretty sound. 'After all I have suffered at the Bashuskys' hands, I want to be there in person to witness their liquidation.'

'A perfectly reasonable wish, Comrade.'

But then the two men were distracted by the riotous reaction of the huge crowd around them. Blotto had just

189

finished his oration with a rousing cry which he thought was 'Play up, play up, and play the game!' (but in fact was 'The Romanovs have returned to take their rightful place as rulers of all the Russias!') and been greeted by an ovation even greater than any that had preceded it.

Twinks's mind was racing with possibilities. She and Blotto were in a worse glue pot than they had imagined. Somehow they had to escape. If only Petrovsky were with them ... He, she knew, would find a way around their difficulties.

Just as had happened when Blotto had willed it in Butyrka Prison, her wish was granted by the appearance of Count Kasimir Petrovsky. Twinks saw him pressing through the crowd, coming straight towards her. She felt huge relief. He, she knew, would rescue them once again.

But, strangely, he appeared not to notice her. Petrovsky walked straight past and greeted Fyodor Vlachko with an enthusiastic handshake. 'Our plan appears to have worked, Comrade!' he said. 'Death to all White Russians!'

# 29

# A Point of Honour

Twinks acted by instinct more than calculation. She rushed across to the Lagonda and said to Corky Froggett, 'Take the top down and be ready to drive for your life.'

'Very good, Milady,' said the unruffled chauffeur.

Then Twinks hurtled across to the space around the microphone where her brother was being fêted and congratulated by ecstatic (and, she now knew, bribed and dissembling) members of the crowd.

'Come on, Blotto me old claw hammer,' she said, 'time for your victory parade!'

He didn't have time to say anything, as Twinks grabbed him by the hand and pulled him towards the Lagonda, now open to the elements with its roof down and Corky in place at the wheel. 'Stand up in the back,' said Twinks, 'and wave like mad!'

Blotto did as instructed.

Twinks then, to the astonishment of their operators, grabbed the camera and microphone which had been recording the Heir to the Tsar's speech and sprinted to the Lagonda. Tossing the camera apparatus into the dickie, she jumped into the passenger seat. The crowd, she noted with satisfaction, had welled around the car, separating them from Vlachko, Yakhunin and Petrovsky.

'Drive like fury!' she said to Corky. 'And wave like mad!' she said again to Blotto.

The chauffeur pressed the self-starter and the great car lurched forward. The crowd parted to make way for them, waving back at the Heir to the Tsar and cheering valiantly.

'Straight for the Polish border, Corky!' cried Twinks, 'And then back to Tawcester Towers as quick as a cheetah on spikes!'

Twinks had told Blotto he could sit down as soon as they had left the crowd outside the Winter Palace and he did so with some relief. He still hadn't a clue what was going on, but felt confident, as ever, that his sister had things under control. And a warm glow suffused his being. He hadn't anticipated that the people of Russia would respond with such enthusiasm to their introduction to cricket. He had the satisfaction of a job well jobbed.

There was quite a strong police presence on the streets of St Petersburg, but they made no attempt to stop the Lagonda at any of their checkpoints. Indeed, they saluted and cheered. The red flag on the bonnet was still doing its stuff.

Twinks's photographic memory had all the maps of the Northern European landmass at her fingertips, so she could guide Corky through the tangled streets of St Petersburg on the most direct route to Poland. All seemed set fair.

But once they had left the city behind and were heading west on the icy open road, Twinks instructed the chauffeur to stop. He did so very gently to avoid skidding.

'There's something we haven't taken into account, Blotto me old bathroom cabinet,' she said soberly.

'And what might that be, Twinks me old egg-coddler?'

'The Bashuskys.'

'But I thought they'd been coffinated. The firing squad. Tough Gorgonzola and all that rombooley, but not a lot we can do about it.'

192

'No. They're still alive. In Butyrka Prison. They're not going to be shot until Fyodor Vlachko can get to Moscow to witness their deaths.'

'Well, I'll be jugged like a hare!' said Blotto.

There was a long silence. Both of them knew that there was only one thing people of their breeding could do in such circumstances. Such things were points of honour for families like the Lyminsters.

'Change direction, Corky,' said Twinks. 'We're going back to Moscow.'

# 30

# Doing the Decent Thing

Once again they drove non-stop back to Moscow, with Blotto and Corky alternating at the wheel. They were glad they had brought the jerrycans of petrol in the Lagonda's secret compartment because they saw no signs of fuel depots on the road.

Twinks's memory guided them through the streets of Moscow until they ended up directly outside the Butyrka Prison. The Hispano-Suiza with its flag of validation was still parked directly outside the grim building.

'Wait in the car, Corky,' she said. 'Keep the engine running. Come on, Blotto.'

As ever obedient to his sister's least command, he got out of the Lagonda. He was of course still dressed in the uniform of the Heir to the Tsar, and the King George false beard still clung to his cheeks.

Twinks led him across to the forbidding main doors of the Butyrka Prison. 'Cross your fingers and tippy-toes, Blotters,' she said, 'and pray to the Great Wilberforce that the guards' rotas work in our favour!' Then she lifted the massive metal knocker and let it clang down on to its metal boss. The reverberation seemed to shudder through the entire building.

The Great Wilberforce – or whichever other deity was keeping a kindly eye on Blotto and Twinks that day – was fortunately up to snuff. The prison doors creaked open to reveal the two people whom she most wanted to see in the world at that moment – the guards, Ivan and Leonid, who had previously escorted them from the holding cell back to their cell to Death Row.

'Behold,' cried Twinks, dramatically pointing to her brother, 'the Heir to the Tsar!'

Ivan and Leonid immediately fell to their knees, crying out praises of their imperial saviour. Both grabbed hold of the Tsarevich's hands and started covering them with stubbly kisses.

'Hey, rein in the roans for a moment!' said Blotto, who had after all been to an English public school and didn't like the idea of boddoes kissing each other on any part of their anatomy. 'There's no need to behave like French gigolos!'

'There is something the Tsarevich requires of you,' said Twinks in a voice horribly reminiscent of her mother's.

'Anything,' said Ivan.

'Whatever the rightful heir to all the Russias commands us to do,' said Leonid, 'we will do it!'

'Then release the Bashusky family from their cells and bring them here!' cried Twinks.

'We will do that, Your Excellency,' said Leonid, not sure what title she should be accorded.

'And we will do it quickly,' said Ivan. 'We have just received a telegram from Comrade Fyodor Vlachko saying that he will soon be here to witness the execution of all the Bashuskys by firing squad.'

'Then go and get them without delay!' screamed Twinks.

While the two guards dashed off into the gloomy interior of the prison, Twinks ordered Corky Froggett out of the Lagonda and into the Hispano-Suiza where he was instructed to start up the engine. 'And you take the wheel of the Lag, Blotto!' she ordered her brother.

The somewhat bewildered Bashusky family were hustled out of the doors of Butyrka Prison by Ivan and Leonid. 'What's going on?' demanded the Count.

'Are we leaving Moscow?' asked Masha in despair. 'I want to go back there!'

Twinks did something she'd wanted to do ever since she'd met the Bashuskys and shouted, 'Shut up!' Then she ordered them into the Hispano-Suiza.

Just as they were getting in, a black Mercedes-Benz limousine screeched to a halt in front of the prison. From the front of its bonnet waved a red flag with a black hammer and sickle on it.

Urging Corky to drive off in the Hispano-Suiza, Twinks leapt forward and with a deft twist of the wrist broke off the thin flagpole on the Mercedes. Then, before Count Kasimir Petrovsky, Fyodor Vlachko and Father Kyril Yakhunin had time to get all the way out of the limousine, she leapt into the Lagonda's passenger seat crying, 'Drive like the wind on wheels, Blotto!'

He needed no second bidding. In a fusillade of flying ice, the Lagonda hurtled off in pursuit of the Hispano-Suiza.

The time it took the Bolshevik conspirators to get back into the Mercedes gave the two other cars a slight advantage, but that was quickly eroded. Although Twinks's recollection of the Moscow road map was perfect, she did not know the network of minor roads and back alleys like the Muscovites in the limousine. Soon the front of the Mercedes was nudging against the bumper of the Lagonda.

But when they reached the first roadblock Twinks's calculations paid off. The Bolshevik guards waved through the Hispano-Suiza and the Lagonda, saluting fervently as they did so. But they weren't about to do the same with any vehicle that didn't display the appropriate flag. The Mercedes was stopped at the barrier and when the people inside it started to argue and bluster about this treatment, they were all arrested.

Meanwhile, the Hispano-Suiza and the Lagonda sped on towards the Polish border. And more than once from the second car ecstatic cries of 'Larksissimo!' and 'Hoopee-doopee!' were heard.

# 31

# The Retreat from Moscow

Once they had crossed Poland and re-entered Germany, they stopped by a bridge over a fast-flowing river. Into it, ceremoniously, Twinks threw the camera and recording equipment that she had seized in St Petersburg. The visual record of her brother's representation of the Heir to the Tsar was lost forever.

There then followed a discussion as to whether they should complete the journey via Berlin or not. The Count and Countess Bashusky were quite keen on the idea – they hadn't done all the shopping they'd wanted to on Twinks's account at KaDeWe. Masha, predictably enough, was miserable because she wanted to go back to Moscow.

Sergei, on the other hand, was absolutely desperate to return to Berlin. If he was not allowed to see Natasha Lewinsky again, he swore he would shoot himself.

Twinks thought the best plan would be for them to separate. The Bashuskys should drive the Hispano-Suiza to Berlin, while she, Blotto and Corky took a more direct route to Calais, whence they could catch a ferry back to England.

The first argument put forward against this plan was that none of the Bashuskys had ever done anything useful like learn to drive. Twinks was halfway through suggesting that maybe Corky would have to delay his return to

Tawcester Towers to chauffeur them when she encountered a totally unexpected objection.

It came from her brother. To her surprise, Blotto sided with the Bashuskys. He wanted to go back to Berlin.

'But why, you clip-clop? You're still a marked man there. What is there in Berlin you want?' Blotto looked deeply embarrassed. Twinks asked in a shocked voice, 'It's not that waitress – or should I say "waiter" – Jutta, is it?'

'No, by Denzil!' replied an equally shocked Blotto.

'Then I haven't a bat's squeak of an idea what ...' And suddenly it came to her. 'Oh no. It's your cricket bat, isn't it?'

Blotto nodded sheepishly.


It was decided that the first port of call should be the Lewinsky mansion. Sergei Bashusky should at least be given the chance to speak to Natasha Lewinsky. And if she refused to see him or if her father hounded them off the premises – which Twinks thought were the most likely outcomes – at least Sergei would have tried. Then he could return to Tawcester Towers and continue to threaten suicide there.

The failure of their primary mission still rankled with both Twinks and Blotto. They had left their stately home with assurances that they'd return there without the Bashuskys, and the prospect of that happening had become more and more remote as their adventures continued.

Blotto and Twinks had never before failed in one of their missions and the knowledge that they were about to do so really hurt. Apart from anything else, the wrath of the Dowager Duchess would be terrible to behold.

Such gloomy thoughts preoccupied both of them as the Hispano-Suiza and the Lagonda drew up on the gravel outside the Lewinsky mansion.

Sergei Bashusky got out of the back of his car and approached the main entrance. He lifted the knocker, but before he had time to drop it, the door opened to reveal a furious Pavel Lewinsky. This time he was carrying a shotgun.

'So, you have come back, you little rat, have you?' he cried in fury.

'I have come back because I love Natasha!' the pimply youth protested.

'"Love" – is that what you call it? Destroying the reputation of my daughter!'

'I do not understand.'

Natasha emerged from the house behind her father. She looked pale but still beautiful. 'What my Papa means is that I am pregnant.'

'Yes!' roared Pavel Lewinsky. 'And she swears that you are the father! Which doesn't say a lot for her taste. Or her morals.'

'It is true, Papa.'

'I know. I wish any other explanation were true, but this is the one I have to come to terms with.' He waved his shotgun dangerously in Sergei's direction. 'You have ruined my daughter and there is only one way her honour can be salvaged. You will have to marry her!'

'I cannot think of anything I would like to do more,' said Sergei Bashusky, sounding, for the first time in his life, rather noble.

Natasha ran from behind Pavel Lewinsky towards the boy and threw her arms around him. 'Now,' she cried, 'we will never be parted!'

'The wedding will have to be arranged very quickly,' said her father peevishly. 'That way maybe we can avoid scandal.'

By this time the other Bashuskys had emerged from the back of the Hispano-Suiza. The Count was smiling a rather calculating smile. 'If our son,' he said, 'becomes an official part of your family . . .'

'Yes?' said Pavel Lewinsky wearily.

199

'. . . then you cannot really afford not to do the honourable thing and provide accommodation to his parents for the rest of their lives, can you?'

'No,' said Pavel Lewinsky miserably.

Though Blotto had elaborate plans of storming the Berlin police headquarters to reclaim his cricket bat, in fact the object was achieved much more simply by Twinks.

Having first concealed her brother in the secret compartment of the Lagonda, she ordered Corky Froggett to drive up to the front doors of the Hotel Adlon. At the reception desk she apologised for their hasty departure some weeks before. Her brother, she explained, was a dangerous lunatic, and she'd had to – at very short notice – take him to a clinic in Switzerland where he would be incarcerated for the rest of his life.

She would now like to pay the bill for their previous visit and to pick up the belongings of her unfortunate brother.

The management of the Hotel Adlon, not caring what she did so long as their bill got paid, were instantly co-operative. From behind the counter they produced the club that, in his lunatic frenzy, her brother had used against some of Berlin's finest policemen.

Having never seen one, they didn't know that the club was in fact a cricket bat.

When they were safely outside the city on the road to the English Channel, Twinks made Corky stop the car to release Blotto from his temporary incarceration.

She handed him the cricket bat.

'Oh, this is pure creamy éclair,' said Blotto.

And he hugged the bat to him, sniffing its reassuring smell of linseed oil, all the way back to Tawcester Towers.

# 32

# Back to the Status Quo

Blotto and Twinks felt that they returned home in triumph, but they wouldn't have known it from the reception they received from their mother. She was not of the generation that believed children should ever receive praise. It would only go to their heads and make them pert.

Nor did the Dowager Duchess comment on the fact that they had returned without the Bashuskys. That is what she had wanted them to do and what they'd said they'd do, so the details of how they'd done it were of no further interest to her.

The other bonus from their excursion was discovered by Corky Froggett as he primped and polished every tiniest part of the Lagonda to return it to its direct-from-the-factory perfection. In the secret compartment, unnoticed by Blotto in his most recent occupation of the space, the chauffeur found the gold bars that Father Kyril Yakhunin had put there for safe keeping (both the ones he'd been given for inventing a Danish Heir to the Tsar and the ones he'd been given for inventing an English one). They made a welcome contribution to the escalating costs of maintaining an estate on the scale of Tawcester Towers.

Blotto and Twinks never heard of the fate of the Bolshevik conspirators who had so nearly ended their lives, but what in fact happened was predictable enough.

After a period of enjoying the corrupt benefits of power and of liquidating their enemies, Fyodor Vlachko, Count Kasimir Petrovsky and Father Kyril Yakhunin were unseated by a new regime who quickly liquidated them.

Nor did news of what happened to the Bashuskys percolate through to Tawcester Towers. Pavel Lewinsky grudgingly brought his new son-in-law into his business, even to the extent of renaming the bank Lewinsky and Bashusky. When things got too uncomfortable in Germany, he moved his entire operation to New York, asserting 'I knew that one day the name "Lewinsky" would be famous in the United States.'

The operation thrived until it was obliterated in the financial crash of 2008. But during their lifetimes Count Igor Bashusky and Countess Lyudmilla Bashuskaya lived high on the hog in New York at Pavel Lewinsky's expense. Masha kept insisting that she wanted to go back to Moscow. But Sergei and Natasha were extraordinarily happy with their many children, and he completely forgot about threatening to shoot himself.

Blotto returned cheerfully to his alternating seasons of cricket and hunting and communed a lot with Mephistopheles.

His brother Loofah meanwhile continued his efforts to impregnate Sloggo with something other than a girl.

Corky Froggett went on with his daily routine of polishing the Lagonda and daydreaming about the fun he'd had in the trenches.

And, though she was far too canny ever to let anyone see it, Twinks for a while nursed a broken heart. For someone of her beauty and intelligence, having men fall in love with her was something of an occupational hazard, but she had felt a great deal for Count Kasimir Petrovsky. And his betrayal had really hurt.

So she distracted herself with a project of translating Milton's *Paradise Lost* into Sanskrit.

And in that way the even flow of life at Tawcester Towers ran serenely on.